SNOWBALLS AND SCOTCH MIST

A Lady Amanda Golightly Murder Mystery

The Belchester Chronicles: Book Three

ANDREA FRAZER

Snowballs and Scotch Mist

ISBN 9781783756476

Copyright © 2013 by Andrea Frazer

This edition published by Accent Press 2014

Other books by Andrea Frazer

DRAMATIS PERSONAE
& PRONUNCIATION GUIDE
(for budding Enid Tweedies)

Guests at Rumdrummond Castle
Lady Amanda Golightly and Hugo Cholmondley-Crichton-Crump – from Belchester
Towers; Hugo's names pronounced Chumley-Cryten-Crump
Sir Cardew and Lady Siobhan McKinley-Mackintosh – host and hostess; Lady M-M's name pronounced 'Shevawn'
St John Bagehot – pronounced Sinjen Badgitt
Ralf Colcolough – pronounced Raif Koukli
Wallace Menzies – pronounced Ming-is
Drew and Moira Ruthven – pronounced Riven
Iain and Elspeth Smellie – pronounced Smiley
Quinton Wriothesley – pronounced Rizzly

Staff at Rumdrummond Castle
Evelyn Awlle – lady's maid to Lady Siobhan, hostess
Walter Waule – valet-cum-butler to Sir Cardew, host
Angus Hamilton – chauffeur at the castle
Janet MacTavish – cook at the castle
Jock Macleod – piper at the castle
Sarah Fraser – lady's maid to Moira Ruthven (guest staff)
Mary Campbell – lady's maid to Elspeth Smellie (guest staff)
Duncan Macdonald – head gamekeeper and ghillie
Sandy Gunn – piper
Beauchamp – pronounced Beecham by everybody, with the exception of Lady A, who favours the original French pronunciation – valet to Hugo Cholmondley-Crichton-Crump (guest staff)
Enid Tweedie – lady's maid to Lady Amanda Golightly (guest staff)

Police Officers
DI Glenister
PC MacDuff

Prologue
New Year's Eve

Lady Amanda Golightly, together with her dear friend Hugo Cholmondley-Crichton-Crump, entered the hospital in Monte Carlo where her mother, Lady Edith, lay gravely ill, at the fag-end of her life. Hugo's face was full of concern, but Lady A's was set in grim determination. As they reached Lady Edith's hospital bed, the nurse slipped discreetly from the room, closing the door softly behind her. Lady Edith, who had faked her own death twenty years earlier, smiled up at her only daughter beatifically, sighed, and departed this world to a place where it would be a very long time before her only offspring could find her again.

'I think she's gone, old girl,' Hugo said, keeping his voice soft and solicitous. He didn't like overt displays of emotion and he hoped Lady Amanda would be able to act with dignity, given the circumstances. She didn't!

'Wake up, you evil old witch!' she hissed, grabbing her mother's nightie and lifting her bodily from the bed to give her a good shaking. 'You can't just send me a message that I'm not an only child, then pop off. I need to know what the hell you meant by that message. How could I not be an only child? I always have been. What did you mean, you secretive old hag?'

'Manda, I think you'd better put your mother down. She's passed over: she's not going to tell you anything now.'

'She's gone on purpose, just to spite me. I need to know what she meant. How am I not an only child?' Lady

1

Amanda's voice had risen in volume, and attracted the attention of the nurse who had just left.

Hearing footsteps, Hugo pulled at her fingers to release their grip on her mother's nightgown, and led her away from the bed. 'There's someone coming, old thing. Best to act with dignity, in the face of tragedy,' he counselled her.

'Tragedy?' she said in a furious whisper. 'If I don't find out what the old bag meant, I'll kill the messenger and consult a medium to confront her; you see if I don't. I must know!'

'I have a letter here that your mother requested be given to you, should you arrive too late to speak to her. I don't know if she's up to conversation,' said the nurse, from just inside the door, an envelope in her hand.

'The only conversation she'll be having is with St Peter, trying to persuade him to let her through the pearly gates, after everything she's done in her devious life,' spat Lady Amanda, still in a fury. 'She's dead!'

'My sincerest condolences on the loss of your mother, Lady Amanda. We've all become very fond of Lady Edith in the short time she has been with us,' intoned the nurse in a sepulchral tone.

'Condolences be damned! Give me that blasted letter, and get on with making the funeral arrangements. I shan't need her body repatriated, as that would make life rather complicated for me, so if you'd just kindly arrange a cremation and send me on her ashes along with your bill, I should be very grateful.'

Lady A's mood had tempered slightly at the sight of the envelope which would, no doubt, contain the information on why she wasn't an only child. With her hand held out, she tried an ingratiating smile, but in Hugo's opinion, it didn't come off, and looked more like an evil leer.

Hugo decided it was time he took over. 'If you would just give Lady Amanda the envelope, we'll get out of your hair. I have a card here, with the details of where we're staying, but I expect we'll be off to good old Blighty tomorrow, so I'd better give you details of how to contact her there.'

'Blighty? Where is this place called Blighty? I have never heard of it.' The nurse was confused. Some words are inexplicable, if one doesn't know the root or the usage.

'We'll be in England,' Hugo added, hoping this was explanation enough and, grabbing Lady Amanda's handbag, which she had dropped on the bed in her fight to resuscitate her mother, he extracted a card and handed it over, along with the one he had picked up before they'd left the hotel.

Back in lady's Amanda's hotel room, she sat and fumed on the bed, as she re-read the letter her mother had left for her, for the fifth time.

'I simply can't believe it!' she stormed. 'It can't be true! It's impossible! This must be some kind of a last sick joke on her part.'

'There are details in there that tell you how to get a copy of the birth certificate. If there's a birth certificate, then it must be true and you're going to have to believe it, whether you want to or not,' Hugo told her, getting a little fed up with her raging at what was obviously the truth.

'But Hugo,' she countered, 'How the hell am I going to live with the fact that Beauchamp is my brother – or, at least, my half-brother? That's just mad!'

'Mad, but true. You'll have to tell him, of course, although knowing Beauchamp, he'll already know all about it.'

'Bugger!' snorted Lady A and went over to the drinks cabinet to pour herself a very large brandy.

Chapter One
Two weeks later

'Oh, Lord!' exclaimed Lady Amanda Golightly, holding a stiff invitation card that had just arrived in the post, in her hand. 'Blast! Damn! Poo! Well, I simply shan't go. I can't face it again, so I shall refuse.'

'What's that, Manda?' asked Hugo Cholmondley-Crichton-Crump, her elderly friend. 'Where do you refuse to go? What can't you face?'

'It's the blasted McKinley-Mackintoshes. They've invited me for Burns' Night. I don't know; my grandmother's sister marries into the family, then her daughter marries one of her McKinley-Mackintosh cousins, and suddenly we're close kin. My mother put up with it, but I never have, and I won't now.

'I haven't been up there since before Mama died for the first time, and I'll be damned if I'll go again – not to that draughty old castle right in the middle of hundreds of acres of Mac-nowhere.'

'Is that the Mac-nowhere in Scotland?'

'Where else?' asked Lady A, crossly.

'And for Burns' Night, you say?'

'Are you getting hard of hearing, Hugo? Of course it's for Burns' Night.'

'So you've been invited to a castle in Scotland for Burns' Night?' Hugo persisted.

'How many times do I have to tell you? That's what I've been complaining about, isn't it? Are you sure you're not losing your marbles?'

Ignoring this last disparaging remark, Hugo replied,

'Oh, Manda; I've never spent a Burns' Night actually in Scotland. And in a castle too. Please say yes and take me with you as your guest. Please, please say you'll accept.' Hugo had always been very susceptible to the skirl of the pipes.

'Oh, really, Hugo, you can't be serious! You want to go all that way, in January, to the wilds of Scotland, just for a haggis dinner?'

'Pretty please, Manda. I'm getting on a bit now, and if they invite you again next year, I might be dead, and never get the chance to do it.' Hugo was adept at emotional blackmail when he wanted something badly enough.

'Don't say that, Hugo! And you really want to go, do you?' Lady Amanda was astounded by the light of enthusiasm in his eyes, and not willing to contemplate a life without his company now, decided she'd better think twice.

'More than anything. For me. Just this once.'

'I capitulate, but you'll owe me big time for this one,' she replied, with a wince at what now lay ahead of them.

'Will there be a piper? And an address to the haggis? And Scottish country dancing? And … maybe some sword dancing?' he asked, as eager as a child promised an esoteric treat.

'Oh, there'll be all of that, and more. There'll be long, cold, stone passageways with real torches flaring along their length, and deerstalking, although the only thing shooting these days are cameras. There'll be gamekeepers and ghillies all over the place, and absolutely everything will be covered in tartan, both dress and hunting.'

Hugo rubbed his hands together with glee, just before Lady A exclaimed, 'Damn and blast!'

'What is it now, Manda?'

'We've apparently got to bring our own butler/valet and lady's maid. Whatever am I going to do about a lady's maid? I've never had one, and I don't intend to start a habit like that so late in life.'

Hugo, noting the 'we've' with satisfaction, suggested, 'What about roping in Enid? She'd probably be game for it. Get it? Game? Scotland? Deerstalking?'

'Hugo?'

'Yes, Manda?'

'Shut up! But you're right. She'd be perfect. I'll get Beauchamp to collect her, so that I can get her exact measurements, then I'll make a call to Harrods and have them send something down. Beauch ... aargh!'

'Yes, your ladyship?' A tall, impeccably garbed figure had suddenly appeared at her side like magic. It was taking some time to get used to the fact that her butler and general factotum was also her half-brother, but she was dealing with it as best as she could.

Neither could see any good reason to change the status quo, as they were both perfectly content with the way their lives ran, but sometimes it gave Lady A a strange feeling, when she asked – or told – him to do something, then remembered that he was, in actual fact, kin.

'I've told you before not to pad about like a cat. You must've taken years off my life over the years, just turning up like that, when I'm about to call you.'

'Sorry, your ladyship. What can I get you?' Beauchamp's voice was exactly as it had been before Lady A had known about their blood kinship, but that was probably because he had known the truth for most of his life, and had just kept it to himself.

'Enid, is what you can get me. Could you just run into Belchester and bring her up here? I want to measure her for a lady's maid's uniform.'

'Is she by any chance going into service, your ladyship?' Beauchamp asked, a little perplexed at this request.

'Sort of, but I'll explain all when she gets here. If she asks, just tell her there's a little holiday in the offing.'

'Yes, your ladyship. Will there be anything else?'

'Not for now, but when you get back, we'll all have a little cocktail to give us a chance to discuss arrangements.'

'The McKinley-Mackintoshes' for Burns' Night?' queried the manservant, a knowing glint in his eye.

'No names, no pack-drill, my man. Now, the sooner you go, the sooner you'll be back, and we can all have a lovely little chinwag about it. But not a word to Enid until she gets here. I don't want her to get wind of what's in the air until it's a fait accompli.'

'You mean you don't want her to suddenly have another engagement that makes it possible for her to wriggle out of it. You just want a chance to bully her before she knows what's coming,' commented Hugo, tapping one side of his nose with a forefinger.

'Exactly!'

When Beauchamp had gone off on his mission, Hugo became lively again, and asked, 'Can we have tartan, Manda? Please. I've always fancied myself in a kilt.'

'We can, but you'll have trews and be done with. I have no desire whatsoever to be faced with your scrawny old legs every hour of the day,' she replied, waspishly. 'And I shall have a long skirt and one of those over-the-shoulder shoulder sash-cum-shawl thingies. I can order those, with accurate measurements, from a little place my old friend, Ida Campbell, uses in Scotland. She's so clan-crazy she's even got tartan carpet; makes me feel quite ill after a while, so I don't visit often.'

'But I don't want trews,' Hugo wailed in disappointment.

'Do you know what's actually worn under a kilt, Hugo? Nothing: absolutely nothing. You'll freeze your wrinkly bits beyond recovery. Do you really want to do that?'

'Not really? Is it so very cold there?'

'Hugo, it's January. It's in the north of Scotland. There'll probably be feet of snow, and the only heating in that humongous stone castle is from log fires, which may look huge, but, if I remember correctly, the heat never reaches further than two feet away from the seat of the fire, and the rest of the space might as well be outside, as far as temperature goes.'

'Hmm.' Hugo took a moment lost in thought. 'I think trews might be a better idea. I don't suppose I can wear a sporran with them.'

'Absolutely not! That would look, to my mind, rather obscene, as if you were … hm-hm,' she cleared her throat self-consciously, 'flying without a licence.' This description gave Lady A a flush of embarrassment, and she hurried on with, 'I'd suggest you pack lots of warm jumpers and your winter underwear, and we'll discuss it further when Enid arrives.'

Enid joined them about half an hour later, and Beauchamp immediately went off to mix some cocktails of sufficient strength to persuade their poor guest that she really wanted to stay in a draughty old Scottish pile, not as an invited guest, but as a lady's maid.

Enid was all of a flutter, wondering why she had been summoned at such short notice, delaying the explanation even further by divesting herself of several layers of clothing before settling on a sofa, eager to hear what was afoot.

Before any explanation could be made, Beauchamp returned bearing a tray with four double tulip glasses on it, handed it round with his usual air of formality, then announced, 'I made Frozen Melon Balls, which seemed rather appropriate, but I used the larger glasses, as the usual size seemed a little – shall we say, unpersuasive.'

'Quite right, too, Beauchamp, and it'll give Hugo pause for thought on the subject of kilts,' Lady A intoned, puzzling the two who had not been party to the conversation about the merits of trews over kilts, then she came over all embarrassed again, as did Hugo himself, at the name of the cocktail, and the thought that they might begin to discuss his private parts as if they were an everyday subject of conversation.

Enid broke the impasse by raising her glass and twittering, 'Chin-chin, everybody, now what am I here for?'

'Chin-chin,' they all repeated automatically, and Lady A, recovering her aplomb, speared her with a steely gaze, smiled a wolfish smile, then asked her how she would like to celebrates Burns' Night in a castle in Scotland where they had their own piper.

Cunning old vixen, her words had Enid hooked immediately, and imagining all sorts of romantic images of what it would be like. 'Oh, I'd love to, Amanda.' For she had been invited to drop the 'Lady' when addressing someone who was now more of a friend than an employer, but that was not to last for long.

'Excellent, but you'll have to start referring to me as Lady Amanda again, and after we've had this drink, I must get you measured for some lady's maid's outfits, if they're to be here before we leave. I'll measure you later, Hugo, so we can get the trews exactly right.'

She had successfully changed the subject, as Hugo declared that he knew his own measurements, and would verify them himself, in private. This was getting a bit near the knuckle again, and he willed Enid to butt in and ask some questions.

She obliged exactly on cue, having sat with a bewildered expression on her face, as Hugo protested about letting Lady Amanda at him with a tape-measure. 'What exactly are you trying to inveigle me into, now? I don't think I like the sound of lady's maid's uniforms. What's going on? What are you planning?'

'I've been invited – it's all right, Hugo, it does say 'and guest' – for Burns' Night, to Castle Rumdrummond. You know, the McKinley-Mackintoshes' pile in the north of Scotland? That invitation I've been turning down every year since Mama and Papa died.

'Well, Hugo really wants to go, as he's never been in Scotland for Burns' Night before. I usually just refuse out of hand, but I've capitulated this year because of Hugo's heart-rending plea. However, the invitation insists that I bring my own butler/valet and lady's maid. And I thought it would give you a nice little holiday, and a change of scenery.'

'Waiting on you hand, foot, and finger. Yes, that really would make a lovely change for me. Just what I've always wanted, to be a skivvy in a cold and draughty building in the middle of nowhere, somewhere in the north of Scotland,' Enid replied, a positive sting in her voice.

'It won't be anything like that, I promise you. You're only going as a maid to help me out, not to actually carry out the duties of a maid,' Lady A told her in her most persuasive voice, before turning to Beauchamp and asking him to refresh the cocktails. He rose, with a knowing wink, collected the glasses, and disappeared into the interstices of Belchester Towers to make fresh drinks.

Unlike Castle Rumdrummond, Belchester Towers was not a magnificent ancient pile, but had been built by one of Lady Amanda Golightly's forebears, early in the nineteenth century, to incorporate every luxury of the day, being updated, as new-fangled domestic fashions became popular, including a rope-pulled lift, when Queen Victoria had such a thing installed in her newly built Isle of Wight home.

This fad of modernisation continued, so that, when Lady Amanda was born, the imposing building boasted electric lighting, central heating and the luxury of several bathrooms, each with its own hot water supply. The fabric of the building had not been neglected either, and it had been kept in good order, unlike Castle Rumdrummond, which had spent a century or more crumbling around its owners' ears, they being landed gentry, and unlike the Golightly family, merely nouveau riche, and therefore more financially stable.

Belchester Towers was of red-brick construction, with a tower at each corner, and had three floors and extensive cellarage. The original folly of a real moat with drawbridge had been done away with long since, and it now boasted a rather more conventional means of entry.

Its current owner was a short, portly woman past retirement age, with startlingly bright green eyes, suicide blonde hair, and a positive mania for good manners, except when it applied to her. She spoke as she found, always telling the truth and shaming the devil.

She had found her friend Hugo mouldering in a local nursing home the previous year. A man whose family friendship dated back to her childhood, Lady Amanda immediately rescued him from his depressing and utterly boring existence, and installed him in Belchester Towers as a permanent resident.

She then set about solving the mobility problems which had been the cause of his original incarceration in such a demotivating dump, arranging appointments with an orthopaedic surgeon, to set in place a plan to replace both his hips and his knees, and relieving him of the financial burden of living alone.

After some initial difficulties, they had settled well together, and Hugo, after the first two operations of the planned surgery, had progressed from a walking frame to a pair of walking sticks, and was much livelier than he had been when she had first come across him again. Their shared younger years rejuvenated both of them, and they were better for each other than any therapy or medicine that could be offered to them.

Enid Tweedie, at one time an occasional cleaner at the Towers, had become more of a friend, and her life had become spiced with excitement in the process. Prior to this change in status, she had been a frequent visitor to the local hospital, always having some procedure or another done. Now she had little time to consider her health, she was much the better for it. She had, as the modern saying goes, 'got a life'.

Beauchamp, whom Lady Amanda insisted on calling 'Bo-sham', declared, equally strongly, that the name in England was pronounced 'Beecham', and this was a constant running battle between them, and had been for decades, for Beauchamp had spent his entire working life at the Towers, employed first by her parents, and now, by her.

During the last, eventful year, a few family skeletons had been evicted from the closet, revealing that Lady Edith, Lady A's mother, had not died in a car crash some twenty years before, but had, in fact, faked her own death and spent the intervening two decades on the Riviera, then finally, in Monte Carlo, where she had died at New Year.

Lady Edith's final revelation had been to reveal that Beauchamp was Lady Amanda's half-brother, courtesy of her late father, and that had really thrown the cat among the pigeons. But they were working it out, slowly adjusting a now very ambiguous relationship, with regards to status, but it would be some time before life returned to anything that resembled the norm and, when it did, it would be a completely different norm from before these unsettling facts had emerged.

Lady Amanda had considered this when Hugo had made his heartfelt plea to be taken to Scotland. Maybe a break in a really dysfunctional household would do them the world of good. Only the truly grotesque could make the merely ugly look beautiful.

The next morning, about ten-thirty, Lady A telephoned Enid's measurements to Harrods, the exact model having been chosen the evening before on the Internet site, with a request for express delivery.

Another phone call connected her to the little shop that provided anything in tartan, right down to tea cosies and tea towels. She gave the measurements for herself and Hugo, with those needed for Beauchamp to have a matching waistcoat, all of the garments to be in the Rumdrummond tartan – dress of course, not hunting. These items would be sent, from stock, by courier, the same day as ordered.

Within forty-eight hours, they were all in these strange garments, admiring themselves and each other, ready to set off for what were, to them, foreign climes. 'Well, I don't think we look too shabby,' exclaimed Lady A, looking round at her little clan. 'What does everyone else think?'

'I still think I should have had a kilt,' sulked Hugo, returning to his previous theme. 'I mean, they do wear such long, thick socks, I don't see how I would have been too cold.'

'You would, if you'd ever felt the draught in their dining hall. It just whistles along at floor level, and blows up whatever you happen to be wearing,' Lady A told him.

'And these trews cut a bit underneath, if you know what I mean,' Hugo continued.

'Take off your jacket and come here,' Lady A ordered him. 'It's only your braces. I don't know, Hugo; why do you find it necessary to haul your trousers up to your armpits, when they're supposed to sit at waist level. I realise how difficult it must be to determine exactly where your waist used to be …'

'I say. Manda! That was a bit below the belt, wasn't it?'

'In your case, that's almost just under your ears,' she informed him, not in the least repentant about her remark, working, the while, on setting his braces at a sensible length, so that his suffering was eased, and he looked a little less like a tartan clown.

'I feel like a cross between a refugee from *Upstairs Downstairs* and a loose woman who does 'thing' for money,' commented Enid, rather grumpily, joining in the round of general ingratitude.

'You'll soon get used to it. You need to be more open to change,' her friend advised her.

All eyes turned to Beauchamp, in his bright waistcoat. Eventually he pronounced on his new image. 'I feel like a right tit,' he pronounced. 'I suppose you're going to tell me that I'll fit in just fine,' he said, turning to his half-sister.

'I think you look darkly romantic,' offered Enid boldly, with an attractive flush to her cheeks, at this unusually forward remark.

'He does, indeed,' agreed her friend, and smirked at her butler, soon to be Hugo's valet.

'How are we going to get there? What are the travel arrangements?' Beauchamp asked, a mistrusting expression on his face.

Lady Amanda took a deep breath and said, 'Hugo and I will fly up on Friday, while you two take the Rolls for us. I'm sure we'll be well looked after while we wait for you, and I can't presume to be lent transport when we get there. Expecting to be provided with a car would be too much of a liberty.'

'And sending us up by car isn't?' Beauchamp's worst fears had been fulfilled.

'It'll be an adventure, and think of all that beautiful countryside you'll pass through.'

'You've only arranged this so that Enid and I can take the huge amount of luggage you want to take.'

'That's simply not true,' his half-sister argued, noticing how much more like siblings they were becoming.

'Liar!'

That confirmed it, but she managed to rake up sufficient grace to ask him, 'You don't really mind, do you? You do love driving so, and you can stop off overnight where ever you choose. I can't go up without a change of clothes twice a day, and I don't want to wear anything twice, or they'll think I'm too old to care.'

'What do you say, Enid?' Beauchamp asked his proposed travel companion.

'Oh, I don't like flying, but a long journey by car will be a treat for me,' she replied, smiling shyly.

'Well, that's all settled then, isn't it? I suggest you go and mix us four Highlanders, and we can all toast our proposed little holiday,' trumpeted Lady Amanda, a smile of triumph splitting her face in two.

Chapter Two

Lady Amanda and Hugo's flight was as uneventful as any other plane journey that doesn't include the unexpected excitement of a crash landing, or a collision with mountains or sea.

The food provided en route was more easily identified by colour, than by taste, and when their bland meal was offered, Lady A ignored what the flight attendant had told her about the two choices on offer, and turned to Hugo, who had insisted on a window seat, and asked him, 'Do you want brown lumps or white lumps?' They'd both taste of nothing, so it was probably best to choose by eye.

'I beg your pardon?' queried Hugo, not used to flying, and in a very excitable mood.

With a sigh, she replied, 'It is alleged that the choice is between chicken supreme and beef stew, but they'll both taste of nothing, so it's just as easy to choose by colour. What may be pleasing on the eye will certainly not be pleasing to the taste buds.'

'I'll have whatever you're having,' he decided distractedly, looking out of the window again, through a break in the clouds.

She had already had to dissuade her travelling companion from having a practice run with his life-jacket, and had rescued him from the lavatory, where he was unable to work out which way the door opened, and had cried plaintively for help, like one of the three old ladies in the 'Oh dear, what can the matter be?' children's song, so she was just pleased that he had found something on the ground to hold his attention.

The brown lumps also distracted him for a while, but she was mightily relieved when the plane landed, feeling great sympathy for mothers who had to travel with small children.

They were met at the airport by an ancient Bentley and an even older chauffeur, a bent old man whose face was as creased as that of a monkey, his head proving to be covered with only tiny wisps of white hair, when he doffed his cap. He introduced himself as Angus Hamilton, tottered around in a haphazard manner while Hugo loaded the bags into the boot, then fussed around them with fluffy blankets, when they were finally settled in the rear of the car.

'How long is the drive?' asked Lady A through the ancient speaking tube, raising her voice sufficiently for it to carry without the tube's aid, as their chauffeur had not proved to have the acutest hearing during their short acquaintance.

After three repetitions of her question, Hamilton considered for a moment or two, then said, 'It should take about an hour and a half, but with the snow, it'll take a wee bitty longer, ye ken.'

There was quite a bit of snow lying around, and although this proved a very pretty prospect through the windows, it was obvious how detrimental to driving it was, as the car slipped and slid in an alarming manner, while Hamilton fought to control the wheel, sitting so low, that he could barely see over the steering wheel.

'The gritters couldnae get oot the mornin', because their diesel was frozen solid,' he informed them in a cheerful voice.

It was a tense drive, Lady A resorting to silent prayers, while Hugo cowered under his blanket like an ostrich burying its head in the sand, and took, not an hour and a half, but nearer four hours. The heater in the car worked in only a half-hearted way, and they were frozen stiff by the time the vehicle crawled up the long drive to Castle Rumdrummond, which had, fortunately, been gritted by the estate workers.

Hamilton seemed not a jot affected by the bitter temperatures, both inside and outside the car, and ,dismissing them as poncy Sassenachs, wheezed his way up to the front door to get someone to help with the bags. As far as he was concerned, his duty was done for he would have no truck with heaving around luggage,.

A suitably attired member of the household staff came out to their aid, and introduced himself as Walter Waule, butler-cum-valet to Sir Cardew McKinley-Mackintosh. 'We dinnae hae a great number of workers in the Castle, so we all double up, as it were,' he explained, rolling his 'r's ferociously. 'Hae ye any staff with ye?'

'We've got a valet and lady's maid arriving by car sometime tomorrow,' Lady A explained.

'That's vera well, as some of the guests seemed tae hae forgotten to bring staff wi' them, and we cannae cope withoot help.'

He showed them to their rooms, explaining that the booming sound they heard as they entered was the dressing bell. The two Sassenachs had hoped to arrive in time for afternoon tea, well over by now, but it was only six o'clock, and surely far too early to be dressing for dinner.

'Dinner will be served at six-thirty,' explained Hamilton. 'The master and mistress like to dine early, so they can get to bed by nine. No need to change t'night, as ye've on'y just arrived.'

Lady Amanda bit her knuckles with distress at this news, and Hugo's face was so long, he was almost trailing it up the stone staircase, as he plodded in Waule's wake. They exchanged a look that said all too obviously: what the hell have we let ourselves in for?

Their rooms proved to be next to each other and had an adjoining door, through which Hugo wandered after only a few minutes on the other side of it. 'I say, Manda! You might have explained exactly what you were getting me into,' he complained.

'Me getting you into? It was you who pleaded like a petulant child to be allowed to come here. I told you I'd much rather have stayed at home. If that man Waule and the chauffeur are anything to go by, the members of staff are going to drive me mad with their accent. That's the Scots all over, though. If they're not rolling their 'r's at you, they're rolling their eyes. It's not easy being a Sassenach up here.

'And it's a dry house. That's not to say that some of the walls aren't running with moisture, but don't expect any cocktails, or wine with dinner. You'll get a thimbleful of scotch on your haggis tomorrow, but apart from that, the only other drink they ever indulge in is a wee tot of whisky at Hogmanay, and then only the one.'

'What?' Hugo was horrified. 'How shall we survive?'

'Don't worry, help is at hand,' announced Lady A, producing a silver hip flask from her capacious handbag along with two small silver beakers. I have brought us enough for two Scotch Mists apiece, and when Beauchamp arrives he has with him a hamper with the necessary ingredients to provide us with cocktails as usual, and a few bottles of wine with which to while away the time between dinner and a decent bedtime.'

'You genius woman,' exclaimed Hugo, eagerly accepting his beaker. 'And we shan't need any ice because this place is absolutely freezing. I shall be surprised if I sleep a wink in this temperature. Hang on a minute, though. If we have no ice and no lemon, that means that the only ingredient left for a Scotch Mist is the whisky. You can hardly call that anything but a straight scotch.'

'Oh, use your imagination, Hugo, and be grateful that I

brought anything at all. It'll be the essence of a Scotch Mist, and we shall just have to pretend. Never fear about the night-time temperature, though. I have four hot water bottles in my case; two each. You can have one at your feet, and cuddle the other. With a little nightcap, you should go off splendidly.'

'You have been here before, haven't you?'

'In spades, Hugo. And, like an elephant, I never forget, especially if my home comforts are threatened. What do you think of your room?'

'More of a dungeon, if you ask me. Tiny windows like slits, so it's probably in permanent twilight even in full daylight. Everything's stone, except for the furniture. The bed's old enough to have had Bonnie Prince Charlie sleep in it, and the draughts – they seem to come from all directions at once. I'm really grateful that you thought to bring hot water bottles.'

Lady Amanda looked towards her bed, a tiny half-tester that must once have been the property of either a midget or a child. 'If I don't lie still in that thing, I'm going to roll off and get a concussion on this stone floor.'

'My bed's so big you could get lost in it. I'll never get the whole bed warmed up in a million years. Just as well you brought your hip flask.'

'I've got another in my luggage with cognac in it, so that we can warm our insides before turning in for the night. There's also a pack of cards and a set of dominoes, so that we don't die of boredom.'

'You might have said it was going to be this grim,' Hugo grumbled.

'I did!' barked Lady A, in self-justification. 'You just saw the romantic side of staying in a Scottish castle for Burns' Night, and never examined the impracticalities. I did say: be it on your own head, but did you listen? No, you bally well didn't!'

'I suppose we'd better go down,' he sighed, using his

sticks to turn towards the door.

'Yes,' sighed his companion. 'Don't want to miss the non-alcoholic cocktails, now do we?'

'Dear Lord!' was Hugo's reply. 'What a beastly thought!'

Pre-dinner drinks turned out to be a variety of very unpleasant vegetable juices, all originating from produce grown on the estate. 'I think mine's sprout,' hissed Hugo, grimacing as he tried the contents of his glass.

'Shhh! Here come our host and hostess. Don't let them hear you maligning their hospitality. Here, she broke off and turned to her right. 'Good evening, Cardew. Lovely to see you again, Siobhan. This is a friend of mine, Hugo Cholmondley-Crichton-Crump. Hugo, please allow me to introduce you to Sir Cardew and Lady Siobhan McKinley-Mackintosh.'

'Room all right?' asked Sir Cardew, shaking hands vigorously with Hugo.

'Comfortable enough?' queried his wife, offering him a hand as limp as a wet fish.

'Thank you very much,' Hugo replied, being careful not to utter the out-and-out lie, 'yes'.

The dining room proved to be a cavernous hall lit by huge flickering chandeliers, a fire burning at each end, but totally failing to project the heat as far as the ends of the long table, some of its length having been removed for the relatively modest house party of just ten guests, no doubt more than just two of them in torment, due to the Spartan state of their accommodation.

'Who are all these people?' Hugo whispered sibilantly into Lady A's ear.

Keeping her voice down, she murmured, 'The names here are going to give Enid forty fits.'

'Go on, then,' ordered Hugo, sounding a bit more enthusiastic than he had since their arrival.

'Well, you've already been introduced to Sir Cardew,' she reiterated, nodding her head to one end of the table where their elderly host sat, his bald head gleaming in the light from the chandeliers, a moustache of immense proportions helping itself, along with its owner, to the Cullen skink they were currently consuming, 'and his wife Siobhan.' She nodded at the other end of the table where their hostess sat, her hair ruthlessly tinted and back-combed into a style reminiscent of the sixties, her face a thick mask of make-up totally inappropriate to one of her years.

'On Sir Cardew's left is St John Bagehot,' she informed him, impelling him to take a quick peek at a terribly refined-looking man who brayed like a donkey when he spoke. 'And he's next to Ralf Colcolough. He's a rather 'naice' young man who's come in place of his parents this year, because the poor old things are both in bed with flu, but he'd no doubt have tagged along anyway.

'Then there're Elspeth and Iain Smellie.' Iain was a small man with a fiercely thick black beard and a mop of similarly-coloured hair. His wife – goodness gracious, Hugo! – was a delicious half-caste, he thought, and whom he would later learn had a Bahamian father. Her wiry hair was caught at the back of her head and held there with a hair clip that looked suspiciously as if it had been made out of knitting needles.

'Next, you'll find Wallace Menzies, making up that side of the table. Siobhan thinks he's hot, so she arranges to have him sitting next to her whenever possible.' Menzies had the almost-black hair and piercing blue eyes of that particular sort of Celt, and was, indeed, capable of being described as almost beautiful. He also wore full Scottish regalia, which the ladies thought enhanced his appearance immeasurably.

'On this side, starting on Sir Cardew's right, is Quinton Wriothesley, known, behind his back, as Grizzly Rizzly –

one look should explain that one. On his right, next to you, is Moira Ruthven, and on mine is her husband, Drew, and that's the lot.'

Moira was a small grey-haired woman who knew exactly how to apply make-up suitable for her age group, and her husband was a tall man with what hair he had buzz-cut to a brutal number one, thus giving the impression of almost complete baldness. He, too, wore full dress tartan, and his sporran gave Hugo a start, as, at first glance, he thought the man had a cat on his lap.

'I shall introduce you to Moira, then I'm going to have a good old catch up with Drew,' she told him, thinking that it was time Hugo let go of Nanny's hand and acted with a little more independence.

'Manda, can I just ask you a quick question? Why do all the guests, with the exception of that charming coffee-coloured lady across the table, speak with upper-class accents? Are they all English?'

'Indeed they are not, Hugo, my dear little innocent. They were all sent to good English public schools exactly so that they would talk like that, and not with the accent of their birth country. Think about it. If you wanted little sonny boy to, one day, have a career in the Foreign Office or the Diplomatic Service, would you choose for him to adopt a Scottish accent, or would an upper-class English one seem preferable?'

'I see what you mean. So what about the little lovely over there?' he asked. 'She sounds decidedly Scottish, although she certainly doesn't look it,' he concluded, indicating Elspeth Smellie with a barely discernible nod of his head.

'That's because she was brought up in Edinburgh, although she did go to a good school, and Iain met her and fell in love with her. Nothing his parents could say or do could sway his opinion, so in the end, they had to give in and give their blessing for the marriage. I rather think her colouring and the accent make a delightfully enigmatic mix.

'Now, may I introduce you to Drew Ruthven, who is the son of a bishop, but still retains an incorrigible sense of humour? Drew, may I introduce a very old friend of mine, Hugo Cholmondley-Crichton-Crump?'

'Crikey, Manda, that's a bit of a mouthful,' he replied, and then turned to Mr-C-C, 'Do you mind if I just call you Hugo? We often use surnames for male guests, but if there was a fire and I had to call you – Fire, Cholmondley-Crichton-Crump! – you'd be burnt to a crisp before I got to the end of your name.'

'See what you mean,' replied Hugo with a smile. 'That's perfectly all right, provided I'm allowed to call you Drew, otherwise I'll sound like I was your fag at school.'

'Heaven forfend. Hugo and Drew it is, then,' agreed his new acquaintance, and they fell into easy conversation about what they could expect from their visit.

Lady A, meanwhile, was gossiping eagerly with Moira, leaning right across Hugo in a most unmannered way, to catch up on news of old friends, and friends who had gone to that great yearbook in the sky. It was as well to know who one could cross off one's Christmas card list, as it was such a waste of a card and stamp, if the recipient were deceased.

As it was announced that coffee would be served in the library – there was no need for the ladies to depart while the gentlemen partook of port, as it was a 'dry' house – Lady Amanda grabbed Hugo by the arm and whispered, her lips not moving, giving a good impression of a ventriloquist, with Hugo as her dummy, 'We'll try the coffee once, but it used to be dreadful. If it hasn't improved, I've got something a little more palatable upstairs and, by tomorrow night, Beauchamp will have arrived with full supplies for us.'

The library was as depressingly stony as the dining hall, with little in the way of comfortable furniture to lighten its atmosphere: what furniture there was being of the hard, lumpy variety that never encouraged one to linger for longer than a few minutes.

Coffee was duly served in plain white, chunky cups and saucers that looked as if they had been lifted, wholesale, from a 'greasy spoon', and the coffee itself dribbled feebly from an urn that had been pushed in on a trolley by one of the castle's staff.

Hugo sipped tentatively at the turgid liquid at the bottom of his cup, thinking that generosity with any sort of fluid wasn't the norm in this household, then his face crumpled with disgust as the liquid hit his taste buds. With a tremendous effort of will, he managed not to spit it back into the cup, but instead, removed a handkerchief from his pocket and delicately coughed into it, thus expelling the dribble of foul stuff from his mouth without losing face.

It had tasted strongly of chicory, with only the barest hint of coffee, and the texture was disconcertingly muddy, reminding him of the old joke that the coffee must be fresh, because it was 'ground' only half an hour ago.

Halfway through coffee, Sir Cardew disappeared and Siobhan explained to the gathered guests that he always went outside after dinner for a little quiet contemplation. It was a habit that he had acquired shortly after they took over the castle following her mother's death, and she was glad of it, in that it gave her time to take in the fact that she was an orphan, and had climbed another rung higher up the mortality ladder.

She also took time to look back at the strange custom of her family, in that inheritance went down the female line, with the husband of the first daughter of the family always having to change his name to Rum Drummond, instead of the wife taking her husband's name. The entail of the estate had insisted upon this practice until she had challenged it when she married Cardew, and had won the battle to have this name-change clause revoked, leaving her husband free to retain his birth surname.

Taking a further sip of the execrable coffee, to ascertain whether it was as ghastly as he had first thought, Hugo took a quick glance in Lady Amanda's direction, as he heard her delicately clear her throat, and noticed that she, similarly, had a handkerchief pressed to her mouth, a frowning forehead showing above its material. Meeting his eyes, as if she could feel him looking at her, she removed the handkerchief and announced that they would be off to bed, now, if nobody objected, as they always retired early at Belchester Towers.

The others could think what they liked about the two of them retiring at the same time. After that explosion of filth in her mouth, she didn't give a damn, and needed something to wash the gritty aftertaste away, as soon as possible.

Hugo trotted along behind her, his sticks almost a blur in his haste to retreat to the tiny corner of Castle Rumdrummond that had become their temporary haven, away from both their hosts, and the rest of the guests staying there. He felt that he might have missed his way in the time/space continuum, and found himself in the middle of a Vincent Price film, where he had no business to be at his age.

Outside, at the base of the west tower, stood Sir Cardew, contentedly puffing his cigar. This was one of the pleasures of his day, and he liked this quiet place. The west tower was the highest of the castle's look-outs, and it had the best view over the most vulnerable flank of the stronghold.

From there, even at ground level, he had a view across rough pasture to the beginnings of the pine forest to the west. To the north he could see the steep climb of the hills, ascending towards the heather of a high moor and, to the south, the land sloped gently down to a river valley studded with little clusters of stone dwellings, their lums reeking tonight in straight spires rising to the heavens, undisturbed by any breath of wind.

The weather was in a state of uneasy calm but, when he was full and contented after his evening meal, this surveying of his land lifted his spirits, and he firmly believed that this aided his digestion and relaxed him before retiring for the night.

Back in Lady Amanda's room, she took the hot water bottles into the bathroom and filled them from the tap, knowing that the hot water could inflict serious burns in the evening, but chill to the marrow in the morning.

A fire had been lit in both rooms, and they moved the one hard chair that each bedroom contained over to the fire in Lady A's room. The clock on the mantelpiece showed that it was only eight o'clock, and Hugo sighed, as he read the story its hands told. 'A few days here is going to seem like a lifetime,' he commented glumly.

'But you'll be able to dine out on the stories for years to come,' Lady A soothed him, 'And tomorrow night, Beauchamp and Enid will be here, and maybe we can make a four at bridge. That'll help to pass the time, although, tomorrow being The Night, there'll be piping and dancing, so perhaps we won't be confined to our chambers so early.'

Before Hugo could unburden himself of a cheery comment at this prospect, the wind suddenly made itself felt by belching smoke from the fire into the room, and he collapsed back in his chair in a fit of coughing. 'Listen to that wind,' Lady A said in surprise, suddenly becoming aware that the noise that had been niggling at her thoughts as they chatted was actually the narrow windows shaking in their frames. 'It's getting wild out there. I'll just take a look out,' she said, putting her head the other side of the curtains.

A few dim lights shone out from the mean castle windows but, apart from that, it was pitch dark, with no starlight and no sign of the moon. 'Thick cloud cover, by the looks of it,' she pronounced, withdrawing from her draughty position next to the glass. 'I shouldn't be surprised if there's snow on the way.'

'Oh, great! There's no way I could face being holed up here for weeks on end,' Hugo grumbled.

'And the castle is said to be haunted,' the bad-news-bringer added. 'Did I tell you about the ghosts?'

'No you blasted well didn't, but I suppose you're going to, as now's the perfect moment, with us marooned here at night, and snow on the way. Go on, do your worst!' he challenged her.

'This place is at least seven hundred years old, and has known a lot of history. Over the centuries, several spectral figures have been reported within its confines. There is a lady dressed all in grey who is purported to walk through the dining hall, but at a slightly higher level than the present floor, and leave the vast room through a door that isn't there any more.

'The bedrooms in this wing ...' but Hugo interrupted her with a little yelp.

'Surely you don't mean these bedrooms?'

'They're exactly the bedrooms to which I am referring. Anyway, to continue: apparently the corridor outside the rooms used to be a good deal wider. It was narrowed in works carried out in the eighteenth century, which was probably the last time anyone really worked on this place, with the exception of the sanitary facilities.

'There is a page who is supposed to walk the length of the old corridor, said to be in search of his master. The corridor now being narrower, means that his route is through all the bedrooms, walking through the stone walls between each, as if they weren't there.'

A howl of anguish sounded from Hugo. 'You know I've got this *thing* about the supernatural. Why did you bring me here, when you knew it was reputed to be haunted?'

'I didn't realise you felt that strongly about it,' Lady Amanda replied, with surprise in her voice. 'I just thought it was one of your little idiosyncrasies.'

'What idiosyncrasies?' Hugo exclaimed, startled that she could think he had anything of the sort.

'Well, I've heard you say 'white rabbits' on the first of every month since you've moved in. If you spill salt, you always make sure to dispose of it over your left shoulder; you never walk under Beauchamp's ladder, and I have noticed that you sleep with a night light on. I thought your disapproval of "ghoulies and ghosties and things that go bump in the night" was like those: just things that you'd always done habitually, but nothing serious. You surely don't believe in ghosts, do you?'

'I'll let you know when I see one,' he replied, inching closer to the fire and carelessly tossing on another log. 'Have you ever seen anything here?'

'Of course I haven't. I'm far too pragmatic to be seeing ghosts. They'd be wasting their time showing themselves to me, and they probably know that, and just don't waste their psychic energy. But my mother always claimed she'd seen every ghost supposed to walk this castle.'

'Thanks a bunch. I was just calming down a bit because you'd never had a sighting, and then you have to go and tell me about your blasted mother.'

'But she would say anything to get attention, and you know that, because you knew her.' Lady A was perplexed by what seemed to be a real fear.

'To tell the truth,' Hugo offered in explanation, 'I've never really recovered from a trip on the ghost train at the seaside, when I was a child. I'll admit to you, as I know it will go no further, that I messed my pants on that ride, and it seems to have scared me for life. I did think I'd got over it, but it would seem not.'

'Come on – let's have some of that cognac. A few nips of that, and you'll sleep like a baby, and if you don't think that's enough, I've got a rather drinkable bottle of red wine that I secreted in my hold luggage, and a corkscrew in my handbag.'

'Manda, you really do think of everything.

Chapter Three

Hugo woke several times in the night, but for a variety of reasons. A nightmare about ghostly apparitions had him awake in a cold sweat; the howling of the wind outside and the resultant smoke from the chimney woke him up coughing; finally, an urgent need to empty his bladder drove him from beneath the covers at five o'clock, giving him just enough time to contemplate the folly of drinking half a bottle of wine, as well as three cognacs, immediately before retiring.

At seven o'clock, he was roused again, this time by the family piper marching up and down outside, playing his bagpipes with infuriating enthusiasm. Hugo took a sudden and instant dislike to the pipe music that had always stirred his blood in the past, when he realised it was not just a quick rousing blast, but a performance that eventually lasted for a full half hour.

Exasperated beyond endurance, he made his way groggily to the bathroom in his dressing gown, and drowned out some of the volume of the music (!) with the running of water and the gurgles and bangs that the ancient water pipes made as they delivered the medium in which he would bathe. He could, after all, stick his head completely under the water, thus deafening himself to everything but the noise of the workings of his own body.

The hot water ran cold sooner than he expected, however, and he remembered Manda's declaration of the night before, that the water was only scaldingly hot in the evening, and was determined, thereafter, to bathe before he went to bed. Maybe the warmth of the water would soothe him into the right state to get a good night's sleep, if the piping devil was going to ply his anti-social trade right outside his bedroom window at the same time every morning during his stay here.

There had been no hot soothing cup of English Breakfast tea brought to their beds, as Beauchamp had not yet arrived, and the tea at breakfast proved as unedifying as the muddy coffee, being both lukewarm and almost too weak to be identified as tea. When Hugo tasted his, then looked at Lady Amanda in accusation, she stated bluntly, 'Be careful what you ask for, Hugo, because you might just get it.'

The meal itself was of a similar quality. The bacon was fatty and over-cooked, the tomatoes from a tin, the eggs with yolks as hard as bullets, and the toast both dry and at the same time limp. There were no sausages or mushrooms, and what there was was offered in chafing dishes that completely lacked the ability to keep food warm.

At the breakfast table, his plate loaded with a selection of the poor fare on offer because he couldn't bear the thought of being hungry as well as cold, Hugo noticed that he wasn't the only one looking groggy from lack of sleep. Others, too, were gazing with bloodshot eyes at the other guests to check their condition, bags appending below their lower lids in protest at the lack of any real rest. Others, however, looked as fresh as a daisy, and this wide difference in the others' appearance led him to ask Lady A about it.

'The ones that have been here before use either ear-plugs, sleeping tablets, or both. I didn't like to offer you any sleeping pills last night, as you always moan so much about the drugs you have to take for the pain in your joints.' Lady A spoke roughly, her conscience troubled that she had not even thought of offering him some of her pills.

'I say, that's a bit unfair, when you knew how scared I was when I went to bed. You could've said something,' Hugo replied, his voice like that of a petulant child.

'I'm so sorry, old chap. I'll let you have some of my sleep bombs tonight. I've brought plenty with me, and if they don't agree with you, you can have my spare pair of ear-plugs for the night after.'

'That's more like it, although I'd like to strangle that damned piper,' he retorted.

'You won't want to, after the hoolie we'll be having tonight. He plays like a dream for the reels and other dances. He's played for the Queen, you know. There aren't many as good as him in the whole of Scotland.'

'Then I shall beg to borrow your earplugs for the occasion. He's very loud. Although, I suppose if I didn't wear them, I might go to bed quite deaf, and then nothing could disturb me.'

'Except for the glowing figure of a spectre leaning over you,' Lady A retorted, with conscious cruelty. It was time Hugo got over his childhood scare, and faced up to his fear like a man, albeit an old one.

Beauchamp and Enid arrived halfway through the afternoon, Beauchamp not a jot worried about the snowfall, which had not been heavy, his companion, Enid, totally relaxed as she had complete confidence in his driving skills, and the weight of the old car to keep them from skidding too much.

Angus Hamilton tottered out to relieve them of the car, and directed them round to the servants' entrance, which was to the east side of the castle, and both of them surveyed the monstrous edifice of the place, both having fairly accurate thoughts as to the level of comfort offered by this huge pile of forbidding stone.

They let themselves in carrying only their suitcases; everything else could wait a while before Beauchamp transferred it to his quarters. There was not much activity at this time of day, because luncheon was over, and it was not quite time to start the preparation of the evening meal. Afternoon tea in this household was only a broken dream confined to the past.

They located the servants' hall by the sound of two female voices raised in anger, and followed this to find a large room with a small number of staff sitting about taking no notice whatsoever of the row, which had now progressed past the insults and curses stage to hair-pulling and scratching.

Taking a look round at the others, who still ignored the fight and the new arrivals, Beauchamp strode across to the two women, now locked in the throes of a bitch-fight, and pulled them apart, holding each at arm's length, until he could extract what the cause of this unseemly behaviour was.

'Behave yourselves, ladies!' he ordered them, his voice slightly raised to gain their attention. 'What has driven you to such disgraceful behaviour? I insist that you explain yourselves.'

An extremely fat woman, who had been sitting quietly knitting, slowly turned round, laying her needlework on her lap, to see who owned this unfamiliar voice, and was intervening on what she considered to be her territory. 'And who might you be?' she asked, looking daggers at the two interlopers, one of which had definitely trodden on her toes, metaphorically. She was the one who meted out discipline, as and when she thought it necessary.

Rising from her seat, she hollered, 'Who the hell do you think you are, molesting those girls like that?'

'And who the hell do you think you are, not intervening in what was becoming a very unpleasant fight?' Beauchamp yelled back at her. It wasn't often that he lost his temper, but the way the two girls were clawing at each other, without a soul to come to their aid, had really riled him.

'I am the cook in this household, and responsible for staff discipline,' she answered, red in the face from the sudden flood of anger at his transgression on to her territory.

'And I am a peaceable visiting valet,' he replied, his dignity recovered. 'I'm with Lady Amanda Golightly and Mr Hugo Cholmondley-Crichton-Crump. And this is Mrs Enid Tweedie, lady's maid to her ladyship.'

He still had both girls at arms' length, and he surveyed them now, as they calmed down. 'Is it safe for me to put you two down?' he asked, 'or will you start up again where you left off?'

'I'll see to them,' replied the obese woman, who certainly looked like a woman who was in charge of all the household food. 'I'm Mrs MacTavish,' she informed him, her own temper also reined in. 'Mary, Sarah: wait in my parlour, and I'll deal with you later when I've welcomed these two to our establishment,' she ordered the two combatants, rolling her 'r's at them, like marbles across the stone floor.

Approaching Beauchamp and Enid, she held out a work-roughened red hand, and greeted them both with, 'Please call me Janet, and I hope we haven't got off on the wrong footing.'

'What was all that about?' Beauchamp asked, curiosity getting the better of him.

'Both visiting, like yourselves. They've been here before, and they always go on like that, so we just ignore them now. Sarah, the big one and lady's maid to Mrs Ruthven, is a Fraser. Mary, the little one, who's lady's maid to Mrs Smellie, is a Campbell. Fraser's always taunting her by saying it was the Campbells who betrayed her family, and therefore they're mortal enemies.

'Mary defends her name by pleading that it was all hundreds of years ago, and nothing to do with her, as well

Sarah knows, but that doesn't discourage her from starting a fight whenever she can. Sarah's impossible, dwelling too much on the past and old grudges, and doesn't seem capable of understanding that it's wrong of her to persecute Mary so, so I just leave them to it. They'll be gone in a couple of days, and peace will return – until their next visit, which I hope is a vera long time in the future.'

'I can see now how tedious it must seem to you all,' admitted Beauchamp. 'Perhaps you would be kind enough to introduce us to the other staff, before someone tells us where our rooms are.'

'Of course. I was distracted by the circumstances under which you arrived. Mary and Sarah you've already had a run-in with. The lady sitting by the fire reading is Evelyn Awlle, lady's maid to Lady Siobhan, although why her mother gave the mistress an Irish name, I've never understood.

'The gentleman leaning on the fireplace cleaning out his pipe is Walter Waule, the master's valet and butler, should the occasion arise when he needs both. The gent sitting at the table tying flies for fishing is Jock Macleod, the piper, and – ah, here he comes now,' she said, as the elderly man who had taken charge of the Rolls entered the room.

'This,' she said, 'is Angus Hamilton, chauffeur of this establishment. Everybody, may I introduce you to Beauchamp and Enid Tweedie, who will be joining us for the duration of the Burns' Night visit.'

'Is this all the staff?' asked Beauchamp, looking around him in wonder at the sparse number of bodies.

'It's Sir Cardew's doing,' she told him. 'He went on an economy drive about two years ago, and got rid of a deal of bodies from the inside staff, and it's been vera difficult to cope ever since. That's why folks ha to bring their aen staff this past two years,' she explained briefly.

There was much shaking of hands for introduction,

before Janet told them where their rooms were, and asked Evelyn if she would be good enough to show them the way, as she was based in the castle. 'And if you would be good enough to direct me to where the car is kept, I have some things to transfer to my room,' Beauchamp requested.

'Angus,' Janet named her victim. Please go out to Mr Beauchamp's car and transfer the contents up to his room, while Evelyn shows them their quarters. They'll need some time to unpack, so I think that's the least you could do for them.'

With a muttered, 'Havers, woman!' Angus vacated the seat he had just taken, and tottered off to do Cook's bidding.

Evelyn led them from the servants' hall down a long corridor, and then up the twisting spiral of an ancient and worn stone staircase, which enjoyed virtually no natural light. Enid squeaked with anxiety, but Evelyn merely said, 'Don't worry, dearie. You'll soon get used to it. You'll probably be up and down enough to have learnt it before tomorrow bedtime.' Her accent was not quite as strong as Cook's.

Enid squeaked again, this time with trepidation, at this awful prediction.

At a quarter to four, a discreet knock on the door of Lady Amanda's bedroom produced a squeal of delight from within, and she hurried away from the hand of whist which she and Hugo were playing, to answer the familiar knock. 'Beauchamp!' she cried, as if she hadn't seen him in years. 'Enid! How lovely to see you. Do come in.'

They entered, Beauchamp carrying a large tea tray which he had filched from the kitchen, the rest of the ingredients necessary to providing afternoon tea now being safely established in his room, including a small camping stove. 'I've taken the liberty of choosing Earl Grey – I have lemon, should you require it – and Enid has the biscuit barrel with some of your favourite thin arrowroot biscuits.'

'Oh, Beauchamp, Enid, seeing you here is like a castaway sighting a ship,' said Lady Amanda with real sincerity.

'Hear hear!' added Hugo. 'This is an absolutely ghastly place, and I can't believe I let Manda talk me into this trip. I can see why she's always been unavailable in the past.'

Lady A gave him an old-fashioned look, but did not defend herself, all present knowing the real reason they had come all this way. Instead, she said, 'Would you please be mother, Enid, dear?' the wording of this request enough to convince anyone of how genuinely pleased she was to see the new arrivals.

Halfway through tea, Lady A, dunking her biscuits in a most vulgar manner, explained, 'As tonight is the big celebration, and they seem to be a bit short of staff, here, since I last visited, I expect you'll both be asked to help out in the dining room. Beauchamp, you'll probably have to take the part of a footman, because of your height, and I expect you'll be asked to aid with the serving, Enid.'

Enid squeaked again. It was beginning to herald the forming of a habit. 'But I've never served at table before in a place like this,' she piped, her voice shrill with anxiety. 'I've never even been in a place like this before.'

'Don't worry about a thing. It's the same as serving at much less grand tables. Just serve everything from the left, and try not to drop any 'neeps' or tatties down any of the ladies' décolletages.'

'Great! Now you've said that, I'm probably going to do it. And what the heck are 'neeps' and 'tatties'?' she asked, wondering what exotic ingredients these could be. She had led a sheltered English life in Belchester.

'Turnips and potatoes, Enid. The Scots have little imagination when it comes to food,' replied Lady A, with a sweeping denunciation of Scottish cuisine in its entirety.

'I won't have to serve the haggis, will I?' she almost squealed, just thinking about the accidents that could happen.

'Absolutely not!' Lady A assured her. 'Cardew always does that. Just don't worry about it and everything will be fine.'

'That's easy for you to say.' Enid would not let herself be reassured.

'Yes, it is, isn't it,' replied Lady A, unsympathetically.

The dressing gong boomed dismally at six o'clock, and the guests departed for their rooms to dress for this, the object of their visit. At least the food would be edible, Burns' Night always considered one of the great celebration days, in this household.

Beauchamp and Enid had been requested not to help them dress, as they had been perfectly capable of carrying out this personal task since they had been children. Lady A and Hugo would be dressing in their new tartan finery, and both paid special attention to their appearances for the occasion. At least the huge grim wardrobes boasted full length mirrors on the interior of their doors.

At six-twenty, the discreet knock on Lady A's door heralded the arrival of Beauchamp and his silver tray, holding only two glasses this evening. Enid floated behind him like a little cloud, a small ice-bucket held with two tea-cloths, to stop her freezing her fingertips. 'What, no cocktail for you two tonight?' queried Lady Amanda. 'And why's Enid carrying a blasted bucket?'

'All will be revealed in due course. I'm afraid we're both on duty, your ladyship, and it would not be seemly for us to appear with alcohol on our breath,' he replied, with dignity.

'I suppose you're right, but there you go 'your ladyshipping' me, again. I am not my mother, you know, and never will be.' Until her mother's death, he had always addressed her as 'my lady'.

'I'm afraid you'll have to accept that form of address, now your dear mother is no longer with us.'

'But you never used it before, when she was supposed to have been killed in that car crash two decades ago,' she challenged him.

'That is because I knew all along that Lady Edith had not died, and that form of address would be wholly inappropriate. Now that we know she is really deceased, I'm afraid I can't help it,' Beauchamp defended himself.

'I suppose it doesn't really matter, if it carries connotations of seniority, in your eyes. Now, what have we got tonight?' she asked, eyeing the contents of the glasses on the tray greedily.

'A snowball for you, m'lady, although, before you protest,' he said, holding up one hand as a look of horror crossed her face, 'it is my own creation, which I have privately named "a turbo-charged Snowball",' he concluded, causing Her Ladyship's face to dissolve into a smile of quiet gratification. 'And for Mr Hugo, I have a Scotch Mist, which I understand is the best medium in which to see ghosts,' he added, with a smug little smile.

'I nearly had one of those last night,' Hugo mumbled.

How on earth did Beauchamp do it? thought Lady Amanda. He couldn't have been aware of a conversation to which he was not privy, but he'd already got to the heart of Hugo's fears about the castle. 'Well done! Beauchamp to the rescue, again,' she said, reaching eagerly for her glass.

'You two look very Scotch, I must say,' commented Enid, eyeing the pair up and down, totally unaware of her pun.

With a sharp intake of breath, Lady A exclaimed, 'Don't you ever use that word downstairs with the staff.' She'd almost said 'other' staff, but had managed to stop herself just in time.

'Why not?' asked Enid, puzzled.

'Use Scots or Scottish. There's nothing the Scots like less than being described as "Scotch". It's all right as a name for their national drink, but not for anything else. Try not to get yourself in hot water. They've a fierce temper.'

'We've already discovered that, Lady Amanda. There were two visiting maids fighting like alley cats when we arrived, and Beauchamp had to separate them.'

'Really? How exciting! What were they fighting about?'

'One was a Campbell and the other was a Fraser.'

Lady A held up a hand to halt Enid's narrative. ''Nough said,' she grinned. 'That old grudge will never be forgotten. If it happens again, take no notice, unless they seem about to break anything other than each other's faces.'

The dinner gong sounded its sinister metal voice once more, and Beauchamp withdrew a slim silver hip flask from an inner pocket. 'That was your summons to dinner, as you are no doubt aware,' he informed them, 'but I have a little corpse-reviver here – a full flask of Frozen Spirits, in fact – in case you are in need of a little tipple before turning in.

'Enid, here, has a small bucket of ice, to keep it at the optimum temperature, and I shall place the two over here, in the draught from the window, to achieve that aim. I, of course, will make sure that your hot water bottles are in your bed at a decent time, and I wish you a very good evening.'

Draining her glass at a swallow, then gasping as the turbo-charged ingredient of the cocktail hit her, she summoned Hugo to join her on their descent to dinner. She had high hopes of this evening, and wished that he would enjoy himself too.

Back in the servants' quarters, there was a state of panic reigning over the absence of Beauchamp and Enid, and their reappearance heralded sighs of relief from all sides. Cook fixed them with a beady eye, and informed them, 'You're on wine duty, Beauchamp, and you're serving at table, Mrs Tweedie.' Enid was too flustered even to attempt to ask her to call her Enid.

'Evelyn and Walter will show you the way to the dining hall, and we all wear sashes on Burns' Night, to show that we're celebrating. Here are yours,' she concluded, handing them the aforementioned garments, which sported a Scottish saltire on both front and back. Beauchamp was already wearing his tartan waistcoat, and felt like a Christmas tree in the process of being decorated, as Enid reached up and dropped it over his head with a little snicker.

The dining hall had been draped with winter greenery, the fires stuffed with logs large enough to completely fill the width of the vast grates, and flaming torches adorned the walls, making the room quite bright and light, and giving it a definite air of being en fete.

As Walter Waule went through the drinks to be served, which, of course, proved not to be wine at all, Beauchamp looked on in disbelief. There was to be a dandelion and burdock to go with the first course, Lucozade to go with the main, and lemonade to help down the dessert.

'What is the first course?' he asked, not quite satisfied with what he saw in front of him.

'Cullen skink,' replied his educator, 'same as last night.'

Beauchamp thought for half a minute, and then suggested, 'Do you not think that orangeade would complement the soup better?'

Walter also stood for a while, lost in consideration, then said, 'I ken you're right, Mr Beauchamp. I'll get it changed right away.'

Beauchamp raised his eyes heavenwards and sighed. He'd be glad to be back in Belchester Towers, where life was reasonably sane – some of the time, at least!

When Lady A and Hugo left their rooms to go down for dinner, they were surprised and delighted to find that the whole length of the corridor to the staircase had been lined with the flares of real torches, much more in keeping with the age of the castle, than the weak electric lights that had guided them to dinner the previous night.

'This is better!' exclaimed Hugo, admiring his trews in the light of the flickering flames. 'I hope the improvement goes on for the rest of the evening, and, if it doesn't, we've always got that flask of cocktail to see us off into the Land of Morpheus.'

'You keep on hoping, Hugo,' Lady A advised him. 'If my memory serves me correctly, the dining hall will be unrecognisable from yesterday evening.'

'Oh, goody!' piped Hugo, his eyes beginning to glow with excitement, and when they reached the dining hall, his eyes and mouth were a trio of 'o's at the transformation that had been wrought since yesterday. It was even warm, the fires being constantly stocked with fresh wood laid in high heaps in the grates, and pumping forth a most gratifying amount of heat.

They took the same places at table as they had before, and Hugo whispered into his companion's ear, 'Why no piper? Seems a bit odd, tonight of all nights.'

'He doesn't appear until he pipes in the haggis, after the first course, but you won't be disappointed.'

'At least he won't be waking me up this time,' Hugo observed, looking smug at this conclusion.

With everyone feeling warm, and delighted in the change in the grim old hall, conversation hummed throughout the first course, not a soul complaining that it was the same as they had been offered the evening before.

The haggis was to be the delight of the evening, followed by dancing.

Lady Amanda and Hugo had quite an audience as the details of their two previous brushes with murder were teased out of them, both adopting a coy attitude and, therefore, making their fellow diners even more eager for details.

When the first course had been cleared, the sound of distant piping was discernible, no doubt emanating from the kitchen, whence the haggis was conveyed to table, and a hush descended on the diners. Lady Amanda took this opportunity to draw Hugo's discreet attention to something she had secreted into her handbag before they left their rooms.

'Oh,' whispered Hugo, his face a mask of delight. 'How sneaky of you,' he commented as his eyes caught sight of the hip flask full of what, no doubt, was cognac. 'I hope it's not lemonade with the main course, or we won't get away with a little slug in our glasses.'

'If I remember aright, it'll be Lucozade, Sir Cardew's favourite tipple, and nobody will suspect a thing, if we add a little extra ingredient, surreptitiously.'

The music grew louder as the piper and haggis grew closer, and the atmosphere of anticipation was palpable. Closer and closer it came, until Jock Macleod entered, his face purple with his efforts, his complexion clashing horribly with his red hair and beard. Behind him waddled Cook, who would not let the honour of carrying the haggis go to anyone but herself. Her face was also a fiery red from her efforts in the kitchen.

Behind her, Enid carried a huge tureen of what Hugo presumed were neeps and tatties, and, behind her, Evelyn Awlle bore a small glass jug of what, he supposed, was the minute ration of whisky, known here as Scottish gravy, for adorning the haggis.

The sound of the pipes was almost unbearable when the

piper was so close to them, but they bore up without complaint, as the haggis was set before Sir Cardew, the neeps and tatties in the middle of the table, and the little jug to the right of the master. An intricately decorated short sword was passed to their host by Walter Waule, and Sir Cardew stood, gazing first at the haggis, then round the table at his guests.

The piping ceased, and the hall was completely silent, waiting for the address that would follow, and really start the celebrations. He took a deep breath, puffing out his chest like a pouter pigeon, and launched into the traditional verse, his voice strong and full of emotion, as he began to recite the age-old words of the Scottish bard, Rabbie Burns.

'Fair fa' your honest, sonsie face,
Great chieftain o' the pudding-race!
Aboon them a' yet tak your place,
Painch, tripe, or thairm:
Weel are ye wordy o'a grace
As lang's my arm.

'I'm glad that's …' whispered Hugo, not getting a chance to get to the word 'over'.

'Shhh!' Lady Amanda hissed. 'He's only just started.'

'The groaning trencher there ye fill,
Your hurdies like a distant hill,
Your pin was help to mend a mill
In time o'need,
While thro' your pores the dews distil
Like amber bead.

'Is that it?' Hugo enquired again, rather fed up with all this stuff he couldn't understand.

'No it is not! Now hush up!'

'His knife see rustic Labour dight,
An' cut you up wi' ready sleight,
Trenching your gushing entrails bright,
Like ony ditch;
And then, O what a glorious sight,
Warm-reekin', rich!

'Is there much more of this?' hissed Hugo, through the side of his mouth. 'I'm beginning to feel that Rabbie was short for Rabid.

'Shut up, Hugo! This is almost sacred in Scotland. It'll be over in a minute, and you'll get to stuff your face to your heart's content.'

'Then, horn for horn, they stretch an' strive:
Deil tak the hindmost! on they drive,
Till a' their weel-swall'd kytes belyve
Are bent like drums;
Then auld Guidman, maist like to rive,
Bethankit! hums.

'I'm considering suicide, Manda.'

'Then commit it quietly, so the rest of us can hear.' Eyes were beginning to turn in their direction, and Lady A was frantic not to be tarred with the brush of someone who chattered all the way through the almost sacred address to the haggis.

'Is there that owre his French ragout
Or olio that wad staw a sow,
Or fricassee wad make her spew
Wi' perfect sconner,
Looks down wi' sneering, scornfu' view
On sic a dinner?

'Oh, come on, this is turning into a joke. And these trews

do chafe so, with no underwear.'

'Be quiet, do! You'll upset everyone.' Pause. 'What, Hugo? You mean you're not wearing any drawers? You fool! That only applies to kilts, not to trews. Really, you are the end. No wonder the seams rub. Now, shut up! Sorry, Moira. Sorry, Drew.'

Poor devil! see him owre his trash,
As feckles as wither'd rash,
His spindle shank, a guid whip-lash;
His nieve a nit;
Thro' blody flood or field to dash,
O how unfit!

'Manda?' Hugo hissed again. 'I can't understand a blasted word the man's saying. What heathen language is he speaking?'

'It's old Scots vernacular English. Now, shhh! If Cardew notices us talking, he'll get himself into a fearful bate.' Another 'shhh' came from across the table, and two Sassenach faces blushed at their overheard interruptions.

'But mark the Rustic, haggis-fed,
The trembling earth resounds his tread.
Clap in his walie nieve a blade,
He'll mak it whissle;
An' legs an' arms, an' hands will sned,
Like taps o' trissle.

'Manda.'

'What now?'

'I need to go. It's urgent. And I really haven't got any knickers on.'

'This is the last verse just coming up, so shut up and hold on to it.'

'But Manda, it's worse than you think. I don't want to

do number twos in my trews and besmirch the noble tartan.'

'Then clench your buttocks and pray, for there's no way I can help you. Now zip it! Your mouth, that is.'

'Ye Pow'rs, wha mak mankind your care,
And dish them out their bill o' fare,
Auld Scotland wants nae skinking ware
That jaups in luggies;
But, if ye wish her gratefu' prayer
Gie her a haggis!'

For a few seconds, silence once more reigned, before Sir Cardew made a slashing cut in the skin of the haggis with the short sword, immediately followed by a further burst of enthusiastic piping. 'Can I go, now?' asked Hugo. 'I really don't think I can wait much longer without doing something very childish on the floor.'

'Be off with you, but get back as quick as you can. Cardew likes everyone present to receive gratefully their plateful of Highland *haute cuisine*.'

Hugo unhooked his sticks from the back of his chair and made off as fast as his arthritic old joints would allow him, while warm plates were provided by Mary Campbell, newly arrived from the kitchen, lest her plates cool too much while waiting for the address to the haggis to finish.

These she placed in front of Sir Cardew, dropping a ghost of a curtsey as she did so, and their host began to spoon the spicy delicacy on to plates, which Walter Waule conveyed down the table to the guests.

It was Enid's job to serve everyone with neeps and tatties from the vast tureen she had carried in. Nervous as a kitten, her hand shook as she spooned the savoury lumps onto the plates, anxiety writ large on her face. She started well, however, and the smiles of gratitude as she heaped plate after plate soon helped her to relax a little.

Everything went well until she came to Lady Amanda and Hugo, as maybe she had relaxed just a little too much by them. As she lifted the large serving spoon to serve Hugo, who had now returned, very much relieved, serving from the left as she had been advised, her arm gave a sudden involuntary jerk, and a large piece of potato shot from her spoon, and for the next few seconds, everything happened in slow motion, in her mind's perception.

She saw the potato sail slowly and gracefully through the air across the front of Hugo's chest. With an almost languid gesture, he reached out a hand, infinitely slowly, and clasped the fingers of his right hand deliberately and almost sluggishly around the loose vegetable cannon.

That was the point where the flow of time returned to normal for her, the spell broken by Hugo's scream of, 'Yow!' as he instinctively got rid of this searing object as quickly as was humanly possible; back the way it came, propelled now by considerable force, coming to rest squarely in Moira Ruthven's cleavage, visible this evening due to her low-cut gown.

She, too, gave a screech of pain, but her quick thinking drove her to pierce it with her fork, before throwing it down on her plate where it lay, innocent and mute. Both ladies at table sat with eyes front, innocently, as Hugo attempted to adopt the same expression, as all eyes were now on them.

Enid, however, did not possess such well-bred 'front' and began to gibber and wail, eventually being led away by Evelyn, to the kitchen, where Sarah Fraser was sent to take her place. Cook was very kind to her, explaining that when she had first waited at table, she had had a similar accident, but hers had involved a whole tureen of scalding soup.

'Dunnae fret, pet,' she advised Enid. 'Anyone can make a mistake, if they're nervous. Now, ye'll take a cuppa tea wi' me, and you can go back after the meal to watch the dancing. It'll all be forgotten by then, ye ken. And the lady will dine oot on the story for years to come, ma girl.'

'What, with only Lucozade to lubricate their throats and tempers?' Enid was near tears at the thought, too mortified to ever look any of the guests in the face again.

Cook winked, and told her, 'They've all got a wee flask aboot them, don't ye worry. There's not a guest here who doesnae ken that if they want a wee tipple, they've to bring their own, and be secretive aboot it. The master may claim this is a dry hoose, but behind his back, it's awash with booze.'

After the meal, the piper moved off into the huge main entrance hall, where the dancing was to take place, while coffee was served at table. Lady Amanda and Hugo refused, on the grounds that it would keep them awake, and shortly all twelve diners followed where Jock the piper had gone before them, Lady A and Hugo lagging a little behind, as they took a sneaky sip each from the flask. They weren't the only ones doing this, as they would discover before the evening was over.

When the company was again assembled, Jock struck a lively reel, in which all but Hugo joined in, Lady Amanda being popular as a partner due to the lack of ladies in the party. There were only four present, and Ralf Colcolough unashamedly claimed St John Bagehot for his partner, neither looking particularly put out by the situation, Colcolough taking the woman's part, while Cook, returning to collect her precious haggis tray, was claimed by the master himself, evening things up considerably, with twelve dancers whirling around the floor to the almost tribal, primitive summons of the pipes.

The rest of the staff arrived and were urged to join in, making four more couples, as a grizzled old man who was the head gamekeeper, and not usually inside the castle, joined in. Only Sarah Fraser stood on the side-lines, but she was a big lump of a woman, with a scowling face, who, therefore, attracted no invitations to dance.

The climax of the evening was to be sword dancing, with Sir Cardew taking on the crossed, gleaming blades. Both guests and staff crowded round as he commenced to fling himself around between the knife-like edges of the swords, and all went well until someone gave Hugo a tiny push in the back, he involuntarily moved forward to preserve his balance, and stepped on the tip of one of the blades.

This dislodged the point at which the two swords crossed, and lifted one of them, Sir Cardew lost his timing, and suffered a nasty cut on the ankle as a consequence. As the blood ran down from his wound, the piper stopped playing, and all eyes were on their bloodied host.

'It was nobody's fault,' Cardew admitted gracefully, nevertheless fixing Hugo with an accusatory stare. 'I'll get it fixed up and be as right as rain.'

This seemed to be the signal for the party to break up, as it was already nearly ten o'clock, and well after the household's usual retiring time. As people began to shuffle around preparatory to going to bed, and Sir Cardew staunched the blood from his wound with a handkerchief, Hugo noticed several people taking nips from flasks, their backs to their host in case they were caught out.

'Come on,' urged Lady Amanda. 'Let's get back upstairs and see what Beauchamp's left for us.'

'?'

'I do hope it's champagne,' she answered Hugo's mute question.

As they mounted the stairs, he asked, 'About that poem thingy – did that lot understand it all, or was it just me being ignorant?'

'They were all in the same boat as you, dear Hugo. When Siobhan's father died and he had to take over the

53

address to the haggis, he was in a muck sweat, for he'd never paid it any attention over the years. It was Cook who taught it to him, word for word, by rote.

'Oh, and don't be fooled by Cook. She's a lot older than she looks, her wrinkles being filled out with fat, and charmingly dimpled she appears too, but she's been here since the year dot, and has been the greatest influence over Cardew as to his occasional Scottishness.

'When he came back here, when his wife's father was gravely ill, he hadn't an idea about anything Scottish, with the exception of Hogmanay. Remember, he was brought through the nursery by a nanny, went off to prep school at eight, ended up in an English university, and came home, eventually, to find himself a complete stranger in the land of his birth.

'Then he married Siobhan, and they eventually moved here. That's when Cook took charge of him and gave him Scots lessons, so he didn't look a complete fool, and the old head gamekeeper took him on for hunting, shooting and fishing, so that he could keep his end up with country pursuits. Her father had been the real thing, being educated at home, and never getting as far as university, but Cardew's father wanted his son to have a better education and not appear overtly Scots.'

'What about the rest of the guests?'

'Exactly the same: part-time Scots, to a man, or woman, with the exception of Elspeth.' Here she gave a little giggle, attributable solely to their pre-dinner cocktail and the wee nips they had had during the course of the evening. 'Look around, Hugo, everyone's as staggery as we are, after all their shifty little nips, for they didn't get like that on Lucozade,' and there was, indeed, a sway to the column of guests mounting the stairs in their wake.

'Oh, excellent! It is champagne,' she declared, throwing open the door of her room and seeing the large ice bucket with the top of a bottle of Veuve Clicquot sticking out of it.

A tray held four glasses, but they had not noticed Beauchamp or Enid, because they had been behind the curtains, looking out at the landscape through the tiny slit of a window. Hearing voices, they withdrew from their semi-hidden position and joined the other two, currently taking seats by the fire, which was burning much brighter than the previous evening, for it had been tended, sporadically although this had been, during the last couple of hours, by Beauchamp, who was a wizard when it came to making and maintaining a fire.

'I took the liberty of requesting an extra load of wood, for what was left in here, and in Mr Hugo's room, was certainly nowhere near adequate to provide enough heat to see you through until the end of the evening, let alone the morning.'

'Jolly good show, Beauchamp,' bellowed Lady A in delight.

As Beauchamp dealt with the champagne's cork, his voice barely mouthed the word, 'Beecham,' but he was heard, nevertheless.

'You'll always be Beauchamp to me,' his half-sister retorted, not able to see his mouth, which formed, but did not enunciate, the words, 'I'm Beecham to everybody else, though.'

'It's snowing again, you know,' interjected Enid, in an effort to dispel an atmosphere before it had sufficient time to form. 'It's heavy, too. If it carries on like this, we'll probably have a foot or so by morning.'

This certainly distracted Lady A, for she replied, somewhat imperiously, 'I certainly hope that will not be the case, as we plan to leave tomorrow, and I will not be imprisoned within these ancient walls any longer.'

'Well, as you're not God, you'll just have to accept what you're given, like the rest of us,' replied Hugo waspishly. The thought of staying where they were any longer than necessary had been the reason for this sharp comment, and he followed it with, 'No offence, Manda. Just stating the obvious. You know what I mean.'

Hugo didn't sleep well that night. His room was undoubtedly warmer, and his hot water bottles well up to temperature, but he only managed to doze fitfully for some hours. At one point he awoke with a start, and fancied he saw a white female face, veiled in black lace, leaning over his bed, like the dead, about to kiss him, then lure him to the other side of the valle lacrimarum.

He became fully awake with a high-pitched scream, a noise loud enough to pierce even Lady Amanda's snores, and bring her to his side, to see if he had suffered some medical problem, or maybe even a fall. She entered through the adjoining door to find him sitting bolt upright in bed, his mop of white hair sticking out in all directions, a look of absolute horror on his face.

'Hugo, you look as if you've seen a ghost,' she declared, taking one look at him and deciding he must have had some sort of a fright, even if it was just a nightmare.

'But I did! I did see a ghost!' he almost shouted. 'It was leaning over me, probably trying to devour me.'

'Stuff and nonsense!'

'No, I tell you, it's true! Take a look out of the door and see if you can see anyone disappearing down the passageway. If you can't, it was definitely a ghost,' he replied, and on this point, he was adamant.

Lady Amanda did as she was requested, but caught no sight of any figure hurrying away from Hugo's room.

As she closed the door again, Hugo had managed to mount his high horse without any help from a leg-up. 'It was a pale woman wearing a black veil over her face,' he stated doggedly, folding his arms to emphasise the point, 'and I definitely wasn't dreaming.'

Seeing his stubborn expression, Lady Amanda didn't try to dissuade him, merely offering to leave the adjoining door open, so that she could listen out for any monkey business.

'You can't hear ghosts,' he declared, 'unless they choose to rattle their chains.'

'Well at least this one didn't do that. If she had have done, of course, I might have heard her, and come rushing to your rescue.'

'There's no point in patronising me. I know what I saw.'

'Of course you do, Hugo. Would you like one of my sleeping tablets? I always get a few from Dr Andrew if I know I'm going somewhere noisy, and I think the seven o'clock alarm-piper's enough to waken the dead.'

'I think I'll take you up on that offer. If she comes back, I'll be sleeping the sleep of the just, and, without chains, she can't possibly wake me for another dose of the supernatural.'

'That's the ticket, old man. I'll just go and get you one. You said you dreamt about ghosts last night, so it's probably just a slightly more realistic attack of that feather.'

Before the sleeping tablet had had time to do its job, however, Hugo let out another high-pitched scream which had Lady Amanda back in his room at the double. 'What is it now?' she fog-horned. 'Another blasted ghost?'

Hugo's face was a mask of terror, as he pointed across to the adjoining wall, his bottom lip trembling with fear. 'There!' he whispered. 'There on the wall! Can't you see it?'

'Can't I see what?' she queried, squinting at the wall in an endeavour to see what had inspired so much terror in her old friend.

Hugo took a deep breath before he could utter the word. 'Spider!' he whispered, beginning to gibber. 'Huge!

Monster!'

Lady A removed her slipper and made a pantomime of creeping up on the unsuspecting arachnid. *Splat!* 'There you are, my lad, the nasty monster's gone to the big web in the sky. Just you hope that it doesn't come back and haunt you for I don't have a ghost slipper with which to hit it. Or its mother comes looking for you,' she added, with a modicum of spite, 'Now go to sleep and let me get some rest myself, or I'll be a wreck in the morning.'

Chapter Four

The next morning both Hugo and Lady Amanda were totally undisturbed by the piper, surprising though this seemed when they awoke. They made their way downstairs to break their fast and, shortly afterwards, the breakfast table was a babble of voices discussing the overnight weather. About eighteen inches of snow had fallen, and Sir Cardew had set the estate's small snowplough out to clear the long driveway to the main road, such as it was.

'We've all been asked to stay on, you know.'

'We've no choice. We'll never get out of here at the moment.'

'Don't tell me! The main road's what we'd consider a lane in England.'

'I can't see a gritter coming out this far on such a tiny road.'

'Did you know the phones are out? And I can never get a signal on my mobile, here.'

'Cardew's got a CB radio, so at least he can order rations to be dropped in by helicopter, if need be.'

'Surely it won't come to that? I've got a very important meeting the day after tomorrow.'

'I should give up hope on that, old fellow.'

A loud shout from the old head gamekeeper, now named as Duncan Macdonald and standing in the doorway, drew everybody's attention. Instead of making an announcement, however, he went over to Sir Cardew and whispered something in his ear, discretion having got the better of him at the last minute.

Their host rose from the table, asking to be excused for a few minutes, as something had come up concerning the estate work. 'I wonder what that's all about,' Hugo said to Moira Ruthven, his table companion to the left.

'Probably something to do with deer stalking. There's nothing he likes better than a good tramp through the snow, with the possibility of seeing some wildlife, although Duncan thinks he's soft in the head, only shooting them with a camera. Says that's not what he trained him for, and that he'd never educated a sissy before.'

'I say, that's a bit harsh, isn't it? Not everybody's infused with bloodthirstiness.'

When he turned back to his place, he noticed that Lady Amanda was no longer at table, and he wondered idly where she had gone, deciding that it was probably a trip to the Jacques, of which she wouldn't encourage discussion on her return, so he just got on with his breakfast, poor fare though it was.

When she returned a very short while later, she had that expression on her face that said: 'I know something you don't'. 'What's going on? What's happened?' asked Hugo, eager for news, but she rebuffed him, merely saying, 'It's not my business to say,' squeezing this out between clenched teeth and pursed lips.

'Come on, Manda. I can keep a secret.'

'Can't tell you.'

Before Hugo had time to go into a huff, Sir Cardew returned with a grim face, called the diners to attention, and said bleakly, 'It is my misfortune to have to inform you that this house is now without a piper.' At that, he turned on his heel and left them with no more explanation of this cryptic comment.

'Manda!' Hugo hissed fiercely. 'You can't just leave it like that! Has the piper resigned? Been fired? Run away? What the hell's happened to him?'

'Shhh!' she hissed. 'Pipie's dead. The snow plough guys just found his body, covered with snow, on the drive.'

Lady Amanda had wasted no time in dragging Hugo from the table of now dispersing guests and steering him, sticks and all, outside, where they discovered an abandoned small snow plough, and an unpleasant hump of blood-stained snow, Duncan Macdonald guarding it from unnecessary disturbance. At what appeared to be the top end of the hump, the snow had been cleared away to reveal the piper's face, blue and frozen from its icy covering.

'What the hell's wrong with his face?' she demanded to know, for there was a bulldog clip on his nose, and his mouth was filled with something currently unidentifiable.

'He seems to have a grand load of haggis in his mouth, and I think it'll be found to be up his nose as well. His mooth had a wee bitty tape over it when I found it, but I pulled it off to restore a wee bit of the puir man's dignity.'

'You shouldn't have done that, Macdonald,' stated Lady A with her innate air of authority. 'He should have been left exactly as he was found. Have you still got the tape?'

'I dropped it there in the snow,' he said, sulky at having been upbraided so.

Picking it up with her gloves, Lady Amanda popped it into her handkerchief and placed it safely in a pocket. Turning back to Hugo, she found him blanching a bit at the blood staining the snow, and she then demanded of Macdonald to know if any injury had been uncovered.

The answer was more unpleasant than they had expected, as Macdonald told them that the plough had only stopped when the driver had become aware of an obstruction on the normally clear drive, and that the maw of the plough had 'done a wee bitty damage' to the body, lying in such a vulnerable position.

'Yuk!' exclaimed Hugo, imagining mangled arms and legs.

'Havers, man! It's only a wee taste of blood. Sure the man was deid when the plough hit him, so he wouldnae bleed like a stuck pig, now would he?' Macdonald said with disgust at such squeamishness.

'Then get the whole man uncovered, Macdonald. How can you tell what did for him if he's still covered in snow?' Lady Amanda was taking charge of things just as she always did, without a thought for whose responsibility it actually was.

'I cannae do that! Whatever would the master say?' Macdonald was scandalised.

'Do as you're bid, Macdonald. It could be a case of bloody murder. How can the authorities be alerted if no one knows how he died? Do as I say and get that snow off the man's body.'

Macdonald, recognising the air of authority in her voice, did as he was bid, and soon they could see the whole length of the piper, stretched out in the snow, the mortal wound that had felled him now visible to the naked eye.

'There's a clear wound in the abdominal area,' stated Lady A, in a steady and unsentimental voice. 'Just turn him on his side, Macdonald – yes, I thought so. The man's been run through with a sword, by the looks of it. It was no knife that made that wound, because it has both an entry and an exit wound, so the blade was long.

'Can you just have a rumble around in his sporran, Macdonald? It seems to have something in it, as it has a bulge, and is not lying flat, the way it would if it were empty.'

Again Macdonald recognised the voice of authority and opened the sporran, but rolled his eyes at her, first, at this unwarranted intrusion into what he considered to be the master's territory. He removed a silver hip flask of what proved to be whisky, with a note taped to it, and looked at his finds quizzically. Already wearing gloves against the cold, Lady A had no compunction whatsoever about asking him to hand over his finds, so that she could examine them.

'Whisky!' she exclaimed. 'And that's my hip flask. Look! It's got my initials engraved on the cartouche! What a damned cheek! Someone's been in my room! What a blasted cheek! But what the devil does the note say? 'A wee dram afore ye go.' What in blue blazes does that mean? Was it a gift, or did the murderer plant it there? And if he did, why? This'll take some investigating, Hugo. We'll have to get together, the four of us, and see what we can come up with. I'll not have my name blackened with the suspicion of murder. Damned brass neck, trying to fit me up.'

Apart from 'yuk', Hugo had not uttered a word, and Macdonald had only reacted to orders due to his innate recognition of, and reaction to, the voice of authority. He now spoke, however, giving it as his opinion that the master should be out here assessing the situation, rather than a couple of his Sassenach guests, giving Lady A a dark look, which she interpreted as due to the discovery of her hip flask in the dead man's sporran.

'Nonsense, man,' Lady Amanda upbraided him. 'Hugo and I have had experience of this sort of thing before, and we know what we're doing. Do you know if Sir Cardew has spoken to the Procurator Fiscal and organised a doctor and police presence?' For a moment she had pleasant visions of solving this crime all on her own in the snowbound castle, emerging as the heroine of the hour.

'He has, aye,' replied Macdonald. 'He has one o' they CB radio jobbies, and he did some speakin' on that afore he told everyone in the dining room. Walter from the indoor staff'll be comin' oot here when the breakfast's done with, to take my place. I'm to round up the outdoor staff so we can clear some o' the ground for the big machine.'

'What big machine's that, Macdonald?' Hugo had finally found his voice.

'Tae bring the doctor and the police, sir,' replied Macdonald, pronouncing 'police' as 'po-liss'. 'They're travelling here by helicopter. It's the only way, when the weather's like this, and ye cannae use the roads.'

'And you're sure you didnae do this? I don't see you running for the hills.'

Lady Amanda treated this last remark with the contempt it deserved, and left him to it, her ears ringing with his broad Scots accent, which seemed, to her ears, ridiculously exaggerated. 'I don't know, Hugo,' she said, as they walked back towards the relative warmth of the castle, 'That's the Scots all over. If they're not rolling their 'r's at you, they're rolling their eyes.

'But who the hell stole my hip flask to use to plant on the piper's body? Someone unauthorised has been in my room, and I intend to find out who that was. If that doesn't turn up the actual murderer, it will probably turn up an accomplice. Hmph!'

They entered through the staff door to alert Beauchamp and Enid that they would be needed for a consultation, and found the staff in little huddles, whispering, conspiratorially, it seemed to them.

The news had also curdled the social order with the guests, and they, too, were sitting about in pairs and trios, muttering to each other. As the quartet headed up the stairs, Lady Amanda commented, 'That's killed the conviviality as well as the piper, hasn't it? I've never seen a bunch of people look so guilty in my life.

'I know people react unnaturally to something like this, Beauchamp, before you remind me of it, but there really is an atmosphere of furtiveness in the air, not just with the guests, but with the staff as well. Is it only an exaggerated reaction to Pipie's death, or is there more to it than that?'

After all the busyness of preparing for and executing the Burns' Night dinner, and their stay being such a short one, Beauchamp did not think he would need to transfer the cocktail ingredients he had kept in his room since his arrival, but with the heavy fall of snow, he had managed to bring them all up to Lady Amanda's room, as she and Hugo were obviously going nowhere fast.

He felt, after even such a short time since his real identity had been revealed, less embarrassed if asked to sit down and join his half-sister for a cocktail or afternoon tea, the feeling of guilt being replaced with one of contentment: that he at last belonged where he lived, and there would be no more secrets or pretence on his part.

He had, however, moved the things for afternoon tea into Mr Hugo's room shortly after they arrived, as he didn't want any of the staff tampering with his cake tin or his supply of biscuits, let alone his half-sister's precious supplies of Earl Grey and Darjeeling, and it was a pot of this latter that he brewed for them, to oil the wheels of speculation, as they discussed what might have happened to the unfortunate piper.

Hugo threw a couple more logs on to the fire, now that they had a decent supply, and the four of them gathered round the hearth with their steaming cups and plates. 'There's one thing to be said about cold temperatures,' ventured Hugo. 'They really stimulate the appetite. I suppose that's because the body has to work so much harder to keep warm, and I've got plenty of body working on that, as have you, Manda.'

'Hugo! Is that a reference to my weight?' barked Lady A, an indignant frown crossing her face.

'I'm only stating that neither of us is emaciated. You never looked like Twiggy, even in your youth; you have to admit that, and I could never have been described as tall, slim, and elegant. We're a couple of "portlies", and nothing can disguise that.'

'I really don't think this is the time or the place to be discussing our body shapes, Hugo. We have a murder to solve, and I've been mulling things over about this place. I haven't been here for some years, of course, but the atmosphere just isn't the same. It used to be a very friendly household. The members of staff – of whom, I might point out, there used to be considerably more – as well as the guests, were always convivial, but there seems to be some tension in the air.

'I know we were all focussed on Burns' Night, but beneath that there was a reserve I've never been aware of in the past. The only people I've really spoken to are Drew and Moira, who were placed with us at table.

'Of course, I've known them for an age, but I've met all the other guests before, with the exception of Menzies, on whom Siobhan seems to have rather a crush, and they've been, on the whole, standoffish. I don't know how you feel about how things are at the moment, Beauchamp. Do you detect a difference from when you last came? I know that was before Mama died the first time, but I missed quite a few visits before that, and you and my parents came on their own. Is it me, or is it the place?'

'I can definitely detect a change in atmosphere, especially if you remember that, when Enid and I arrived, there were two maids trying to tear each other's hair out downstairs, and not a soul made an effort to separate them.

'Cook would never have tolerated that in the past. She'd have given them a severe reprimand, and reported their behaviour to their respective employers. Had they worked here, not only would they have been reprimanded, but would have had their employment terminated, as well. Now, she doesn't seem to care much about anything.'

'Everyone seemed really happy when they were dancing last night,' interjected Enid, innocently.

'Did you see the dead look in that maid's eyes?' asked Beauchamp, who was very observant. 'That big lump of a girl that no one seemed of a mind to dance with?' he clarified, with an interrogatory inflexion in his voice. 'Well, that's the look that a lot of the residents of this house seem to possess at the moment, so I definitely think there's something amiss here.'

'The food's certainly not as good as it was before, and I can't be sure whether that's down to the staff, or the quality of the ingredients, but the place is definitely less convivial than it used to be. Although many of the staff have changed, that never seemed to matter before. Cook would wear her bonhomie like a crown, and radiated it over everyone within reach of her. Now, she seems more introverted. I think I'll try to get her on her own and ask her what's happened to alter things.'

'You could have a "wee chat" with Macdonald, too. I don't think he's comfortable in the company of women,' suggested Lady A. 'Enid, you can do your worst with the rest of them, and Hugo and I will make great efforts to ingratiate ourselves with the guests, as we're all stuck here for a while, and not just because of the murder.'

'Oh, by the way, when Hugo and I were outside ...' Here, she gave an account of her and Hugo's discoveries out at the scene of the crime, concluding with, 'And they've notified the Procurator Fiscal, and a doctor and a representative of the police will be arriving by helicopter. The outside staff have been summoned to clear a piece of ground for it to land.

'I just wish we had dear old PC Glenister here. I'm really going to miss his inside information and cooperation. He's become quite one of the gang, even if he does work for that sour-faced Inspector Moody, and he always used to tip us the wink if we needed to know anything.'

'Just be pleased it's not old Lemon-Chops who'll be

working on this murder,' Hugo exhorted her.

'No,' she said. 'With our luck we'll probably get Inspector McLemon-Chops, his Scottish cousin, or something similar. But let's lighten the atmosphere a little. I have, in my handbag, a list of the current guests, and I'm sure we'd all enjoy it immensely if Enid would care to attempt to read it to us.'

'That's me,' Enid declared, 'always the clown,' and she prepared to be ribbed mercilessly when she couldn't decipher, with any accuracy, all the ridiculous names that people of Lady A's acquaintance seemed to own.

The sound of an approaching helicopter was discernible just before noon, and a landing place had been prepared for it in an area of pasture not far from the castle. A route to the castle already existed, in the form of the track that had been cleared by the estate workers to access the landing area so that they could remove the snow, so Macdonald was sent up there in a decrepit Land Rover to meet both medical man and representatives of the law.

Lady Amanda, eager to get a head start, in case the Scottish lawmen were resistant to her charms, began to infiltrate the cliques that had formed, dragging the hapless Hugo in her wake for, although she knew Moira and Drew Ruthven, and had kept in rather sketchy touch with them, there were those in attendance that she had not seen for two decades, and one she had never met before.

She proceeded on the assumption that, if she spent some time working on her acquaintanceship with Moira, she could subtly coerce her into introducing her round those she had not met for so long, and provide introductions to Menzies, whom she had never met.

Moira, pleased with the attention, picked up the subliminal message that Lady A was furiously beaming at her, and proceeded to do just as it was hoped she would, starting with Wallace Menzies, who was sitting chatting in the cathedral-like space for which drawing room seemed such an inadequate description, with the Smellies, the room providing many groupings of seating to fill its vastness.

Elspeth announced that this was the first time they had attended for many a year, but they'd just felt like a little break after the hectic chaos that was Christmas with their large family. She, too, was of the opinion that the atmosphere had changed in some subtle way since they had last attended.

Although her husband seemed to be in agreement with this opinion, saying that some of the conviviality had gone out of it, Menzies, who claimed – untruthfully, in Lady A's opinion, otherwise why didn't she recognise him – that he had not missed a Burns' Night since he was a 'wee laddie', opined that it seemed exactly the same as it always had done, to him.

Lady A immediately concluded that a change would not be noted, if it were subtle, by someone who never missed the January visit, if that were true, but was much more likely to be apparent to someone, like herself, who had not been for several years, and she made a mental note to seek out the Smellies later, to have a chat about how they thought things had changed, in the specific.

Seeing that they were on the move again, Moira materialised at their side and steered them over to a trio speaking in low tones, away from the fire and the rest of the others. Here, she and Hugo were formally introduced to Quinton Wriothesley (Grizzly Rizzly, when he was the subject of a conversation in which he was not involved), Ralf Colcolough (Kooky Koukli – ditto) and St John Bagehot (Bedbug Bedsit – ditto).

Lady A learnt within minutes that two of them had some sort of tenuous connection with the estate, but having made her a gift of that nugget of information, they then turned the subject to the death of the piper.

'Damned rum thing to happen when one is visiting, I must say, knocking off the household piper,' Bagehot opened the subject, his eyes darting round his little group as if he harboured suspicions that one of them might be responsible for the deed.

Hugo picked up on this, and his face became an indignant mask. 'Surely it must have been some outsider who had a grudge against him.'

'Who says it might not just have been a heart attack?' interjected Moira, re-joining the group. 'Playing the pipes is not easy. It required a lot of strength and energy just to get a note out of the beastie. I know: I've tried.'

'Because we've seen the body,' Lady Amanda informed her, 'and he'd been run through with a sharp implement. Of course, this being a castle, with weaponry displayed all over the walls, the first supposition is that it was a sword, but I might be wrong.' She wasn't needlessly giving away inside information; more, she wanted to see what effect this titbit had on those present which, with the addition to Moira, had become the main group in the room.

'And there was something rather odd in his sporran,' she added, wickedly, then nodded to Hugo as she observed the faces around her.

Hugo took his cue with a smile of gratitude on his face. He didn't often get to impart information of this import. 'There was a small flask of whisky in it, and a piece of paper with 'a wee dram afore ye go' written on it. God knows what that means, but the police might be able to make something of it.'

'And it was handwritten, not printed,' added his partner in sleuthing, just to get things nicely stirred, 'So I expect they'll bring in a handwriting expert.'

'I don't think we should let any of that worry us,' soothed Moira. 'It must be some sort of falling out he had with one of the estate staff, or someone from the local town. It can't be one of us; we're all civilised people, with impeccable upbringings and backgrounds, and all that good stuff.'

'Hear hear!' added Drew, in support of his wife's irrefutable logic, and the group began to melt away and glide into other formations and combinations.

When there were just the two of them again, Hugo asked Lady A if she had learnt anything from their little bombshells. 'Only that there are a good few poker faces around here,' she replied, as someone tapped her on the shoulder.

It was their hostess, Lady Siobhan, just bursting with news. 'Spit it out, old girl,' urged Lady A, as the other woman looked like she might burst if she didn't speak soon.

'There's to be a wake,' she announced. 'I know that nobody's going to be allowed to leave until the police are satisfied, so we're going to have a wake for our poor, dear piper, the day after tomorrow. It's going to be for staff and guests. We'll have it in here, with whisky and a buffet.

'Oh, don't worry,' she reassured them, as Hugo's face had taken on a stricken look. 'It won't be rowdy. There'll be dancing, of course, and stories about him told, but there'll be another wake for him with all his family. This is just a gesture to show how much we appreciated him, and mourn his passing.'

'But I haven't a black tie with me,' bleated Hugo, feeling seriously underprepared for an event such as this.

'No need for anything like that, Hugo, dear. This will be in full highland gear, and what you wore for Burns' Night will be absolutely perfect. It's just a celebration of his life, and having a last good time for him.

'And as for tomorrow, do, please take advantage of any of the facilities offered by the estate. There'll be deer stalking, if anyone's interested, a horse-drawn sleigh ride for the less energetic, and even skiing lessons, should anyone feel the urge. There's a great piece of ground at the back of the castle that makes a perfect nursery slope.

'I'll put three pieces of paper on the dining table so that people can put their names down for what they'd like to do, then I'll liaise with the policemen, so that we can coordinate keeping him happy with interviews, and keeping everybody else busy and amused.'

'Have you met the policeman who's going to be in charge of this case?' asked Lady A, thinking: know thine enemy.

'No yet. He and the medical chappie are ensconced in Cardew's study as we speak, but, thank God the phones are on again, so we're back in touch with the outside world again. It's such a bore, only being able to speak to people with CB radios – all that 'breaker, breaker' nonsense, you know. They're a bunch of nuts, in my opinion. Oh, by the way, I think he wants to speak to you first, Manda, due to it being your hip flask found in Pipie's sporran,' Siobhan finished before wandering off to see to her lists.

'I do wish she wouldn't plaster her face with so much make-up or wear her hair in that ridiculously out-of-date fashion,' she said to Hugo. 'She'd look ten years younger if she just got a decent haircut and applied just the teeniest smear of make-up. She's got no chance with our handsome Menzies, looking the way she does: although Cardew's probably quite happy about that.'

An hour later, in Lady Amanda's room, a fierce argument was raging, Beauchamp and Enid both in attendance, but keeping well out of it. 'I want to do a sleigh ride, Manda,' wailed Hugo.

'You can want as much as you like, Hugo. You're going skiing, and that's that,' countered Lady Amanda, her hands on her hips and her head raised autocratically.

'And do I get little skis for my walking sticks?'

'You get ski sticks, you silly old fusspot.'

'But, why can't I go on the sleigh ride? I bet you're going to.'

'I certainly am not. I'm going deer stalking.'

'You're what?' cried Hugo, aghast.

'I've got a fair idea of who's going on the sleigh ride, and the interesting ones will be either deer stalking or skiing. The sleigh won't be out for long, and Enid and Beauchamp can do their darndest to find out about the ones who have selected the sedate option, whom I think will be Siobhan, Drew and Moira.

'Surely, between the two of us, we can get in a few pertinent questions on our excursions?'

'On the way to hospital, you mean?'

'Hugo, don't be such a wet blanket. They know what they're doing. I should think everyone on this estate can ski, given the weather conditions in these parts, and the number of years most of them have been coming here.'

'If I break a leg, I shall find some way of suing you.'

'Hugo, you won't even break one of your beautifully trimmed nails,' she informed him, in the tone of voice that brooked no more argument.

A discreet knock at the door revealed Walter Waule, who requested that Lady Amanda accompany him to Sir Cardew's study, where the inspector was waiting to question her. Hugo was to go down when she returned, followed by Beauchamp and Enid, the four people most likely to have placed the hip flask where it had been found. It was, at the moment, a very incriminating object.

Lady Amanda's knock on the study door was bold, as befitted an innocent person whom someone was trying to frame for a murder. A not-too-strongly accented voice bade her enter, and she went in and was waved to a chair. 'Lady Amanda Golightly?' enquired the broad-shouldered man sitting behind Cardew's desk, a notepad sitting before him, and Lady A was glad there were no 'r's in her name for him to mangle.

'That is correct.'

He rose and held out a hand, saying in his soft Scottish lilt, 'Pleased to meet you. I'm Inspector Glenister, here to find the murderous cur who made away with Jock Macleod …'

She held up a hand to stop him and asked, 'I don't suppose you're any relation to a young PC of my acquaintance, in Belchester. I know the odds against it being a close relation are pretty long, but I have to ask.'

'That'll be my nephew Adrian, if I'm not mistaken.'

'Nooo! What a coincidence! We've worked on two cases together so far – unofficially, of course,' she informed the inspector.

'Aye, I know. He's told me all about you. Apparently you give him a little light relief from that miserable lump Inspector Moody.'

Lady Amanda sighed deeply with relief. 'Then you'll know that I'm simply not the murdering kind,' she said, relaxing a little.

'Aye, that is so. And now I'll share a little secret with you. My PC MacDuff is such a miserable and sulky soul that we refer to him at the station as PC Moody, so my nephew and I have a matching pair, as it were.'

'Is he here with you?' she asked, staring round the room, as a knock sounded on the door, which she had thoughtfully closed behind her, to ensure privacy.

'That'll be him now. Come in, MacDuff!'

A portly young man in uniform entered the room, his face a picture of misery. Even his uniform seemed to droop in sympathy with him. He sidled across the study, avoiding making eye contact with Lady A, and sat himself in a chair away from the desk, with his own notebook at the ready.

'Before we start,' began Lady A, relaxed now she knew she was in safe hands, 'Is Glenister a Scottish name?'

'It certainly is, m'lady.'

'Do call me Manda. It'll make things so much smoother. Now, what do you want to know?'

'I want to know when you last saw the deceased. I want to know how your hip flask got into his sporran, and I need to ascertain that you are not, in fact, a killer,' he told her, smiling broadly at the thought of his interviewee wielding a sword.

'To your first enquiry, I hadn't seen Jock since last night, when he piped for the haggis and the dancing. About the hip flask, I haven't the faintest idea. I do know that it means someone's been going through my room, and that makes me feel cold all over. As to the third piece of information you require, I can definitely confirm that I am not the murderer. Gosh! This is beginning to feel a bit like a game of Cluedo. Lady Amanda – in the snow – with something very long and sharp. Wrong!'

'Do you know of anyone who had a grudge against, or harboured any bad feeling, towards Jock?'

'Not if you don't count the number of guests here who were not over fond of his seven o'clock reveille on his pipes, no,' she replied. 'The last time I was here, his father was the piper, Jock Senior, so this is the first time I'd come across him. I say, have you found the weapon yet?'

'Aye. It was taken from a wall display, used on Macleod, wiped, rather inexpertly I might add, as we found blood on the wall where it was hung, having been replaced whence it had come. I got MacDuff to bag it up, and it's gone off in the helicopter with your hip flask.'

'Oh, by the way,' she informed him, 'Did you sort out the bulldog clip and the haggis?'

'Naturally. This is not my first murder investigation,' he replied with a smile.

'I'm perfectly sure of that, but did Macdonald tell you that there was tape over his mouth when he uncovered the poor man's face?'

'No, he didnae. This is news tae me. And what exactly happened to this piece of what might be vital evidence?'

Lady A was grateful for a short speech that contained no evidence of 'r's. Putting her hand carefully into the handbag that she had, naturally, brought with her, for no lady goes anywhere without her handbag, she removed her handkerchief, within which the incriminating piece of tape rested.

'I think this is what you require,' she announced, with a smug little smile. 'Be careful. I know Macdonald just pulled it off, but I lifted it by a corner while wearing gloves, and immediately placed it in my handkerchief for safety. You never know, it might still contain some useful fingerprints.'

'Ye're a marvellous woman! Adrian was right about you. And we've got a murder bag with us, so we can test for fingerprints right here in the castle,' he crowed, taking the proffered square of material, and handing it to MacDuff, to place in an evidence bag.

'Tell me, Inspector, how come your nephew has no trace of a Scottish accent?'

'My brother moved south not long after I joined the police force. He said it was not a fit job for a red-blooded Scotsman. Adrian was born down in England, and was fascinated with mystery stories when he was a child, and murder stories as a teenager.

'With an uncle already in the police force, it gave him, I think, the extra push to do what he wanted to do, which was join the force himself. He'd been having a bit of a hard time of it with yon Inspector Moody, until he met you, but he says you've brightened up his working life no end. He phones regularly, to let me know how he's getting on.'

'Ah, so he was brought up in England. That explains it. Now, if you've finished with me, shall I send down Mr Hugo Cholmondley-Crichton-Crump?'

'Oh, that is his name. I was wondering if it was a bit of a misprint, it was so long. And dinnae fash yersel'. There's no reason why MacDuff here can't go and fetch him. And when I've spoken to your party, which I believe consists of four persons, then MacDuff here will be well practised for the rest of the summoning. Very pleased to have met you, ah, Manda.' Not only did he remember to address her informally, as previously bidden, but he also went completely overboard on 'very', as if using the extra rolls of the 'r', like an impromptu drum roll, for emphasis.

'Just a word before I go,' she said, as MacDuff disappeared on his errand. 'Has Siobhan, by any chance, given you a guest list?'

'She has, that,' he replied, wondering where this was heading.

'I think you need to be forewarned because, after all, forewarned is forearmed,' she replied, taking the list he had picked up from his desk.

Inspector Glenister had listened to Lady Amanda's pronunciations of the various names with a growing look of disbelief on his face, now and again shaking his head, as he repeated each name, and an occasional shake of the head at the ridiculousness of the situation. At the end, however, light dawned, and he and Lady A shared a conspiratorial smile. 'PC MacDuff' she said pointedly.

'PC MacDuff,' he repeated, his face breaking out in a gleeful grin. 'I think I might enjoy this afternoon more than I anticipated.

As she left the study and headed for the stairs, the gong for luncheon sounded, so she betook herself off from the entrance hall and towards the dining hall instead. Inspector Glenister would have to wait for his next three interviewees until after they had eaten. As she was crossing the hall, she noticed Mary Campbell's frail figure staggering towards the dining hall under the weight of a great tureen of soup, Macdonald standing by the doorway, observing, but not anxious to come to her aid.

Taking herself off to help the girl, when she returned, she noticed that Macdonald was still standing where she had last seen him, as if waiting for a crash, or the sound of breaking china. Suddenly irked by his lack of gentlemanly response, she went over to give him a bit of a talking to.

'Couldn't you have stirred your stumps and given the poor girl a hand? She's very tiny, and not really strong enough to deal with the dish she was sent through with,' she enquired, still wearing her autocratic manner like a diadem.

'I'll nae lift a finger fer a Campbell,' he replied curtly. 'They're traitors, every last one o' them.' His accent was definitely thicker than Glenister's.

'Oh, come on, Macdonald. That was four hundred years ago,' she chided him, referring to the Massacre at Glencoe.

'That makes nae difference, lassie,' he responded.

'But, Macdonald, it wasn't your personal blood that was spilt, was it?'

'Now, I'm gonna tell ye this just the once. 'Twas Macdonald blood that was spilt there, and Macdonald bone that was smashed. I was bred from that blood and bone, and that makes it my blood.

'We took them in, and offered them our hospitality. They broke bread wi' us: they took whisky wi' us. Then they rose like the very Devil himself from Hell, in the night, and slaughtered us.

''Tis Campbell blood that ran in their veins; aye, and 'tis Campbell blood that runs in her veins, the same noo as it was then. I'll no dae it, m'lady. I'm sorry, but I just cannae bring meself' to.'

Lady Amanda walked quietly away without reply. She was not only shocked by the naked hatred in the old man's voice, but really shaken that such a strong feeling could have survived for centuries, and still walk abroad.

Over lunch, Lady Amanda related the tale of what had happened in the hall, and her host and hostess were not surprised at all. 'We went to an inn one night, having been caught out by the weather, and deciding not to continue our journey till morning,' Siobhan began, obviously relating a tale to back up what Lady Amanda had just told the table.

'We stopped at this quaint little place which looked just right to shelter from the storm. Well, there we were, standing in this sort of foyer place, shaking our umbrellas and taking off our mackintoshes, when I heard Cardew 'harumph', and when I looked up, he was staring, and pointing to a sign that said, in large red letters, 'No Campbells'.

'I thought it was some sort of joke, but Cardew told me not to say a word when we went in, for if they found out that we knew any Campbells, they'd not let us stay. The sign was deadly serious. That's how high feelings still run, even after all these years.'

There were murmurs round the table, to confirm that she was not the only one who had come upon such open hostility to the surname and, for a moment, Lady Amanda thought how strange and tribal Scotland still was, in comparison with England, and she longed to be in Belchester Towers, in front of a blazing log fire, eating muffins and butter, and sipping a soothing cup of Darjeeling.

After what passed for coffee in this household, the other three prepared for their interviews, Lady A letting them stew, hugging the secret that the policeman was a relative of PC Glenister on their own patch. She'd had to stew. Nobody could have told her; so she kept it to herself, waiting with good humour, for the wigging she would undoubtedly receive, when they came out.

While they were otherwise occupied, she began to float

around, a second cup of the disgusting brew in her hand, casually getting into conversation with whomsoever she could, in an effort to find out as much about her fellow guests as she could.

She did not include Moira, Drew or Siobhan in this exercise, as she had no suspicions of them, and she also wrote Cardew off as a non-starter, as he'd hardly invite a bunch of folk to his home for Burns' Night, then murder his own piper. That way, madness lay, as far as she was concerned.

She found the effete Ralf Colcolough reading an old edition of *The Scotsman* by the fireside, and sat down next to him on the sofa, in her brashest manner. 'Hello,' she said, brazening out her unlooked-for interruption to his reading. 'How do you know dear Siobhan and Cardew?'

Ralf, too well brought-up to rebuff her, launched reluctantly into how they had met. 'It was about ten, maybe twelve, years ago, and I came here for the shooting – a little party got together by the office. When I got here, I wasn't too keen on killing things, but I found that Cardew and I got on like a house on fire. We're both very keen photographers.

'In fact, it was I who persuaded him not to stalk deer to kill them, but to photograph them. He was bowled over with the idea, and immediately invited me to come back on my own, so that we could try it out. His gamekeeper was furious, but it wasn't Macdonald's call. I've been visiting regularly ever since.'

Writing him off as a useful source of gossip, after half an hour of listening to him drone on about the technicalities of photography, she excused herself and went in search of another victim. This time she espied Wallace Menzies and Quinton Wriothesley at the other end of the room, apparently engaged in earnest and animated conversation.

Hastily pouring the contents of her cup into a pot plant,

then swanning over to the coffee table to refill it, she sauntered over to them and, without waiting for them to notice her, interrupted with, 'I was just wondering what you two gentlemen thought of what happened to the poor piper. I'm sure you're both gentlemen of the world, and must have a much more sophisticated outlook on things than poor, parochial little me.'

Both regarding her crossly, Menzies lifted an eyebrow, lifted a lip in a sneer of contempt, and announced that, as they did not mix with the working classes, they had no idea how they behaved. Wriothesley – Grizzly Rizzly – nodded in ill-natured agreement, and suggested she speak to the staff, who, being those sorts of people, understood their motives much better.

'Do you have no ideas, yourselves?' she battled on bravely, in the face of intense lack of interest and hostility.

'There're plenty of pipers in Scotland. Cardew will easily replace him.'

'That's not the point, though, is it?' Give Lady A her due – once she had her teeth into something, she would not give up easily. 'His father before him was piper to this household and, if we checked, we'll no doubt find that his father before him held that post, as well.'

'And your point is?' asked Menzies, most objectionably.

That was enough for Lady Amanda. 'I offer my apologies,' she said, in her loftiest voice. 'I was of the opinion that I was conversing with gentlemen. Obviously I was mistaken.' And with that, she turned on her heel and stalked off, determined to speak to Siobhan about the people she invited into her home as guests.

While Lady Amanda was thus engaged, Hugo was re-summoned for his interview with the inspector, which he approached with some misgivings. He was, after all, in a foreign country, and didn't know the ways of the natives.

A ringing voice bade him enter Cardew's study, and the gloomy-faced constable followed him into the room, taking a seat along the back wall. After the inspector had greeted Hugo, the constable turned a delicate shade of puce, and dropped his face into his notebook. That wasn't how he had pronounced the old gentleman's name at all. How could he have been so wrong, unless his list was full of spelling mistakes?

When the inspector had introduced himself, Hugo became much more amenable and, after a short discussion about the unfortunate demise of Jock Macleod, Glenister asked him if it was really true, that his nephew had actually discovered him hiding in a downstairs privy, in darkest night, in a house that was not his own.

'I tried to act casually, but I don't think he was convinced,' Hugo replied in all seriousness.

'He told me he also found your partner-in-crime hiding behind the sofa. Is that true as well? I thought he was making it up.'

'True as I'm sitting here in this tutu,' said Hugo, then smiled his ingenuous smile. 'We were caught red-handed, trespassing on someone else's property, without their permission, and your nephew had the kindness just to ignore us, and let us get on with whatever it was we were doing. The woman's case is coming up shortly. If I were the judge, I'd direct the jury to bring in a verdict of justifiable homicide.'

'Adrian thinks you two are priceless, and hopes he's got so much get-up-and-go at your age.'

'I wish I had so much get-up-and-go at my age,' replied Hugo, with unintentional humour. 'Investigating does rather keep the old noodle ticking over, though. If I'd stayed where I was, before Manda rescued me and welcomed me into her own home, I expect I'd be dead by now. Give him our regards when you speak to him, and tell him to call round for afternoon tea, or a cocktail, when he's not on duty. It must be very tedious for him, working for someone as miserable and mean-spirited as Inspector Moody.'

'He does find it rather trying at times,' replied Glenister, with a small smile, remembering the swearing that had carried along the telephone line, the last time he had spoken to his nephew.

'I say,' Hugo asked, in a small voice, 'You don't really suspect Manda, or one of us, do you?'

'I don't, so don't waste your worry on that. I've a feeling the answer to this one lies closer to home than you four.'

Beauchamp was next on the list, followed by Enid, and both these interviews were amiable and polite, Glenister having no cause to suspect that they could ever have met the piper before, living where they did, and had already confirmed this with Sir Cardew.

His nephew had described them all to perfection, and when he had finally met them, he felt he already knew them. He had absolutely nothing to worry about on the Belchester Towers front, and knew that, if he needed anyone to spy for him, or ferret out something, it was one of this crew that he would choose.

Meanwhile, Inspector Glenister's afternoon was getting better and better. He had made a copy of his guest list and given it to the gloomy and taciturn MacDuff, requesting that he bring the guests to him in the order listed if possible. The constable had already fallen foul of Cholmondley-Crichton-Crump, but restored his confidence with Beauchamp (who answered to any variation of his name, if good manners necessitated) and Tweedie. He would not make a fool of himself again.

MacDuff had sloped off, once more, to do his inspector's bidding feeling slightly more confident, and leaving, as was his habit, the door open, and his superior to mutter, 'Born in a barn, that laddie!' The door to the cavernous drawing room, in which the guests were lurking, having taken coffee, was open and, the acoustics were such that Glenister could hear every word uttered by his constable, who had one of those booming voices redolent of doom.

He heard him find his first interviewee, and the request to come to the study, followed by an audible puffing and blowing from the recipient of this request. When MacDuff reached the study door and presented his first 'catch' with the words, 'Mr Wriothesley, sir,' the bubbling of suppressed wrath finally erupted.

'You ignorant little oik! M' name's Rizzly, not that ghastly strangulated noise you made? Have you no education whatsoever, man? Rizzly! That's pronounced R-I-Z-Z-L-Y, for your information, and be sure you don't forget it!'

MacDuff muttered a confused apology, blushing to the roots of his helmet, which he had retained, due to the temperature inside the castle, and he took his place ready to take notes with a very sheepish expression.

It was all Glenister could do to suppress his mirth, and the incident raised his spirits considerably. Working with MacDuff always left him feeling gloomy and depressed, and this was a considerable improvement on normal circumstances.

MacDuff's next mission was to collect Ralf Colcolough, and his first mistake was to raise his voice to ask if that young man was present. At this point, the figure of a young man suddenly swooped down on him, braying, 'Koukli! Koukli! Koukli! *Raif Koukli!*' and the constable actually ducked, thinking he was being attacked by a madman.

From his unseen desk, Glenister turned purple with glee. If MacDuff were to be habitually gloomy, then he'd give him something to be gloomy about.

A request for a Mr Smellie and a Mr Menzies variously brought forth shouts of, 'Smiley, man! That's Smiley! How dare you call me smelly!' and 'Ming-is, you moron! How can you not pronounce Ming-is when you're a Scot?'

By the time MacDuff got to Drew and Elspeth Ruthven and St John Bagehot, he was nearly on his knees with embarrassment, and adopted the policy of approaching the nearest person, indicating the name on the list of the person he wished to collect for interview, thus avoiding using a name at all.

What surprised him most of all was that the inspector had seemed to know the exact pronunciation of each and every one of these truly weird names, and he almost, but not quite, suspected that a practical joke was being played on him.

The Belchester Towers Four reassembled in Lady Amanda's room for afternoon tea, each with a tale to tell of their interview with the unexpected Inspector Glenister. Hugo was the first to speak. 'You might have said something at lunch, Manda. That way, we wouldn't have been in such jitters about the experience.'

'Why should you three get off lightly, when I hadn't had that advantage?'

'Oh, that's rather bad form, don't you think, Manda?' he asked.

'If you want to hear about bad form, I'll tell you about what happened to me while you were being interviewed. There are some uncouth louts, who are under this roof in the guise of guests, over whom I would not pour a bucket of water if they were on fire.'

'Whatever did they say?' asked Beauchamp, fluffing up his dander for possible later use. No one was going to mouth off his half-sister/employer without him having a say in matters.

'It's simply not worth repeating, Beauchamp. I merely

advise you that I should be obliged if you would try to find out a bit about that bounder Menzies, and that cad Wriothesley.'

'Consider it done, m'lady.' Beauchamp was grinding his teeth as he agreed to this. The slightest step out of line, and he'd scrag them, he was compelled to announce.

'Control yourself, man. You'll scrag no one until I tell you to. Have you got that? Now, about tomorrow: I've taken a look at the three lists, and have decided that Hugo and you, Beauchamp, will go skiing, I will go deer stalking and, if you don't mind, Enid, I'd like you to stay in the castle to see what you can screw out of the staff. Do you mind staying here?'

'There's no way I want to go out in this weather. I'll be one big chilblain the day after. I can't think of anything I'd like better than to sit in the servants' hall with that roaring fire, drinking tea all day long, and gossiping to my heart's content.'

'Deal!' yipped Lady A, spitting enthusiastically on her hand and offering it to Enid to seal the deal. Enid declined the hand with a slight shudder, covering her moue of distaste discreetly with her hand.

Chapter Five

The next morning, the three groups gathered together in the hall, waiting to commence their chosen activities. Drew and Moira Ruthven and Siobhan had, as Lady Amanda had predicted, chosen the sleigh ride option, as had St John Bagehot (surprisingly) and Elspeth Smellie, whose exotic complexion would look magnificent in the snowy surroundings.

The stalking group would be led by Macdonald, and included Sir Cardew, Wriothesley and Menzies. Those headed for the nursery slope for the skiing were being led by Iain Smellie, who was an experienced skier, and had volunteered to teach kindergarten today, along with Beauchamp, the rather effeminate Colcolough, and the terrified Hugo.

The stalking party would take with it, or have delivered, a picnic lunch, to be eaten in one of the many shelters scattered around the estate in which estate workers, or anyone else on the property who fell foul of the weather, and needed somewhere to seek sanctuary, could retire. Each contained a table and chairs, a camping stove and a rude cot, in case the weather was persistent in its inclemency.

The sleighing party was the first to leave, warmly wrapped in fur rugs and thick woolly hats, each with its own bright bobble nodding on the top. The stalking party stood at the large hall table surveying a map, Macdonald advising the route that he thought would be the most likely to result in good view of stags, given the latest information he had gathered from other estate workers.

When approved, he marked the route on the map with a bright pink highlighter and, checking that they all had on walking boots and sufficient layers of clothing for the exercise planned, they set off. Lady Amanda, like the other members of the party, had a stout stick with her, to aid walking on the rougher ground, and had made a point of putting on two pairs of long 'janes' and two thermal vests, under her overgarments. No way did she want to become today's case of hypothermia.

Apart from Cardew and Macdonald, her only other companions were Menzies and Grizzly Rizzly, and she muttered constantly to herself to remember not to call him that to his face. The last thing she needed on a day out like this was a smack in the mouth to add to her miseries, and she was determined to gain the trust of these other two guests, to see if they could have had anything to do with the piper's death.

The skiing party headed out to the back of the castle, where there was a room that contained all they needed for their outing. Granted, the skis were not the most modern, but there were boots aplenty, in a variety of sizes, and skiing outerwear too, so that no one unexpectedly joined the Frostbite Club, and went home missing a finger or toe or two.

When each member of the party was clad to Iain Smellie's satisfaction, he warned them not to do anything they had not expressly been instructed to do, and to obey instructions to the letter. Carrying their skis, a somewhat difficult task for Hugo, as he had brought along his walking sticks, as an aid to balance in the treacherous snow, Iain led them to a promontory not far from the rear of the castle, and pointed out the slope that lazily meandered its way down towards the foot of the distant hills.

'This is what we're going to be working on today,' he announced and, in a flurry of skis, ski poles and walking sticks, all of which seemed to have a life of their own, Hugo raised a hand and asked, 'And having got down, how do you propose we get up again? I'm no spring chicken, and don't fare very well with "up".'

'Already taken care of,' answered Iain, a twinkle of satisfaction in his eyes. 'I've made arrangements with Macdonald that one of the estate workers will bring a Land Rover to the base of the slope – he should be with us within half an hour – and he'll convey us back to the top. In the meantime, we'll concentrate on the basics, if you wouldn't mind clipping your boots on to your skis.'

Beauchamp came to Hugo's aid, and ordered him to stand as still as he could, while his boots were offered up to the ski clips. Having been released from carrying the skis, Hugo ditched the walking sticks and used the ski poles, dug well into the compacted snow, to do his best impression of a flamingo, with just one foot on the ground. Finally he was ready, and Beauchamp attended to his own boot clipping.

'Right then, everybody, the first thing we're going to do is just try a gentle movement downhill. You won't need your poles for this. I just want you to turn the toes of your skis very slightly towards each other when you face the slope, before moving on to it. This should allow you to move slowly forward and downwards. If you want to stop, move the tips of the skis closer together. I shall now demonstrate.'

This, he proceeded to do, with perfect aplomb, making it look easier than walking in the snow. 'You first, Beauchamp. You look like a fairly well co-ordinated chap. If you can do it, it will inspire confidence in the others.'

Beauchamp was good at following instructions to the letter after all the years he had worked for Lady Amanda, and managed a slow glide down the shallow first section of the slope, even managing to turn himself sideways and crab-walk back up to where the others were waiting.

'Have you done this before?' Iain asked, surprised at how effortless the man had made it look.

'Never,' replied Beauchamp with a smirk, 'but I have seen it done on the television.'

'Now,' said Iain, 'I want you to have a go, Mr Colcolough, if you would be so kind. Please don't go any further than Mr Beauchamp here did, as the slope gets steeper, the further it goes. And keep to the right side, if you will, for the left side extends much further than the right, and gets a might steeper as it runs. We want to stick to the tried and tested nursery run today.'

Ralf Colcolough, a gangling mess of ski sticks and skis, his long arms and legs seemingly in the control of a malign god, managed to move himself to the top of the little slope with trepidation, frequently making little squeaking noises of fear and alarm.

'No ski poles, if you please, Mr Colcolough. You simply don't need them for this first exercise.'

Colcolough discarded his poles with rather more effort than was necessary, which immediately set him moving downwards. 'Points of skis pointing slightly inwards, please,' shouted Iain, in vain, after his retreating figure.

Gathering speed at an alarming rate, unable to do anything about changing his skis from a parallel position, Colcolough began to wave his arms in the air, and hoots of distress could be heard as he careered towards the bottom of the right-hand side of the slope.

At the foot, where the ground levelled out, he lost control in his panic, and went head over heels, shedding his skis as he went, and proceeding to produce a long drawn-out screech of a word that Hugo pretended not to understand to be 'Ffffuuuuuuuuccckk!!!' just as a Land Rover approached the prone figure.

From the top of the slope, the others watched while the ghillie got out of his vehicle, calmly collected both skis and put them in the back, then went to Colcolough's aid, pitching him back upright and inserting him in the passenger seat, as if pandering to a frightened child.

Back at the top of the slope, the ghillie exited the vehicle first, informing them all that, 'It's just a wee bittie bruising. He'll be fine after a nice long soak. Nae worries.'

Colcolough eased himself out of his seat and said, in apology, to the others in the group, 'I say, I'm dreadfully sorry about what I yelled on the way down. Frightful language. No call for it. Please accept my word that it won't be repeated.'

'Your turn, Mr Cholmondley-Crichton-Crump,' announced Iain, determined that everyone should have a go at this new activity, for he had no intention of letting Hugo wriggle out of it. 'Now, let's get you in position,' he ordered, pushing the hapless Hugo across the snow like an over-sized toy.

'I don't think I want to try this,' he pleaded, but Iain was having none of it.

'I'll just give you a little push, and off you'll go. Nothing to it. Skis turned in a bit, like I told you.'

He'd already given Hugo a mighty shove before he noticed that Hugo still had his ski poles in his hands, and yelling, 'No poles for this,' made a mad grab at them, which destabilised him sufficiently for him to land face down in the snow, watching Hugo's retreating figure from ground level.

'Oh, Lord. Oh, my good gracious me!' exclaimed Hugo, wildly waving his poles, his speed increasing by the second, and his path drifting left. There was absolutely nothing he could do about it, as he approached the steeper left hand side of the slope, and he was aware of Iain shouting, 'No, no! Go right! Turn, you silly old fool. Turn right, for God's sake!'

Even through the buzzing panic in his brain, Hugo was aware of the insult, and thought, as he careered along, his poles waving wildly like antennae, that if he survived this plunge, he had a good mind to beep the blighter on the snoot. Shoving him like that was, if not exactly attempted murder – at least, it wasn't murder yet – but constituted an assault upon his person which was reckless, to say the least.

At this point, one of his ski poles made contact with the ground and catapulted him into the air, where he did a perfect somersault, then seemed to cartwheel towards the far distant end of the steep incline, making 'ooh' and 'argh' noises, with the occasional 'ouch' and, from a distance, doing a fair impression of a centipede on speed.

Before Iain could get to his feet, the Land Rover was off down the slope in pursuit of the flying figure of Hugo, who was just coming to rest in a heap of limbs, skis and poles, lying like a tangled spider at the base of the slope, shouting repeatedly, 'Bum! Bum! Bum!' then proceeding to laugh hysterically.

'Ha ha ha! Hee hee hee hee hee! Ho ho ho!' floated upwards, unimpeded in the cold clear air, to the others in his party, who could not work out whether he was hysterical with fear or had lost his mind somewhere on the way down.

Iain, in a complete fluster lest Hugo try to slap some sort of law suit on him, pushed off and skied down to join the Land Rover, from which the ghillie was just emerging at the foot of the slope. Both men reached the still recumbent form, Iain arriving in a shower of powdery snow as he made an abrupt halt as near to the figure as he could, without actually causing any further damage.

'Are ye hurt, man?' asked the ghillie, showing his concern by casually rolling a cigarette.

'Ha ha hee hee ho ho ha ha ha!' chortled Hugo, still unable to control what sounded like hysteria.

'Do you need an ambulance?' asked Iain, still concerned about litigation.

'I'm fine!' Hugo finally managed to splutter. 'All these

clothes you made me wear. I might as well have been wrapped in cotton wool.'

Pulling off a glove, he wiped tears from his eyes and continued, 'I haven't had so much fun since my first ride on a rollercoaster. Just don't ask me to do it again. Has anyone got a flask about them? I could do with a "wee nip" to settle my nerves.'

At that moment, Beauchamp slid to a stop beside them and provided Lady A's second best flask, the first one now being considered as a piece of evidence in the piper's death, and Hugo took a long, grateful swig. 'I shall refrain from mentioning anything about your mishap to her ladyship, should I happen to see her before you. She'll only fret.'

'Good show, Beauchamp! Excellent idea! I say, do you think I could be dropped back at the castle? I could do with a bit of a lie down, and just ignore lunch. I'm not in the least hungry. It must be that adrenalin stuff that I've heard so much about, and now I think I've experienced it, too. I don't want to do any more skiing, though. It doesn't feel half as elegant as it looks, and I really don't think it's for me. Sorry.'

Lady Amanda's excursion started in what, to her, seemed a slightly bizarre fashion. Heading to exit the castle by a side entrance, the party came upon a pile of what looked, to her ladyship, to be a pile of old tennis racquets. 'Surely we're not playing tennis in this weather?' she quipped.

'Dunnae be so silly, girl!' growled Macdonald. 'The area immediately around the castle has been cleared of snow, but we've tae get tae the forest, and the snow's knee-deep. We'll not get there at all if we dinnae use snowshoes. Noo, get yerselves shod, and we'll be off.'

After about five minutes of puffing and blowing – some had considerable 'corporations' to bend over, to achieve this shoeing activity – the five souls braved the biting cold and went outside to start their trek to the forest, where the snow would be negligible because of the tree cover.

Lady Amanda's gait resembled that of a person auditioning for a part in a live action version of *The Wrong Trousers*, as she lifted her feet high and stepped forward, occasionally getting the back of the snowshoe stuck in the snow. After a few occasions when she nearly took a tumble, she was given an impatient instruction from the morose Macdonald.

'Lift yer feets and plant them down flat, wuman, else ye'll go arse over tit, an' at your weight, I'll nae be pullin' ye up again.'

Insulted to a degree she had only ever before suffered at school, she blushed as brightly as a robin's breast, and did 'as she had been bid', finding that – damn and blast it – the old man was perfectly correct, and it did make the going much easier. None of the others had suffered a similar problem, so she assumed they had used such ungainly contraptions before. At least now she could keep up with them.

At the edge of the forest, Macdonald called them together, so that he could explain what they were going to be doing, for the benefit of anyone who had not engaged in this sort of activity before. As he said this, he glared malevolently at Lady A, and she blushed anew.

'We'll enter the forest in silence. Any communication after that will have to be in signals, or in low whispers of the lowest kind. If we're near a deer, we'll draw attention to ourselves immediately, they have such sharp hearing. We'll be walking against the wind, so that the deer don't smell us coming. That way, we have the best chance of getting some fine photos of the grand creatures.' There was a minute pause while he sneered. He much preferred to stalk with guns. 'Is everybody ready?'

Four heads nodded in unison, each of the party heeding his instructions not to speak, and they entered the gloomy confines of the pine forest, with a final warning given in a whisper. 'Watch out for twigs. They can snap with a crack that would warn every beast of the forest of our approach, in which case we might as well return to the castle and give up. They're canny beasties who like their privacy, and to see them and be unheeded by them is a rare privilege, ye ken?'

Lady A had a feeling that she wouldn't be very good at this. Although unexpectedly light on her feet for dancing, in general she had a poor sense of balance, and tended to be just a tiny bit clumsy in everyday life, to which Beauchamp and her not-quite-complete sets of glassware would bear witness.

As the forest began to close in behind them, she looked back longingly at the pile of snowshoes they had discarded, and wondered if she should give up her plan of trying to eavesdrop on conversations at lunchtime, for that would be the only opportunity, if Macdonald didn't impose a code of silence upon them even while they were eating.

Maybe she should just let them get on with it, and wander around on her own for a while, before returning to the castle, which was, at least, a few degrees warmer than the outside. As she stood, deep in careful thought, a stag strolled across her vision, and she had to clamp a hand across her mouth to stop herself yelling out to the others.

She was downwind of it and, with no inkling of her presence, it sniffed the cold air, shook its antlers in a way that seemed to indicate its joy at being alive, then trotted off into the cover of the trees.

With a sigh of deep pleasure, Lady A smiled a smile of deep appreciation, as if she had been granted this close-up view as a blessing, then nearly jumped out of her skin as a voice at her shoulder whispered, 'What a beautiful wild creature!' Hand clamped over her mouth once again, she turned as quickly as she could, to find Beauchamp, smiling contentedly, just behind her.

'How many times have I told you not to do that, Beauchamp?' she hissed, still conscious that she should make as little noise as possible. 'Anyone else would have trodden on a twig, but, oh, no, not you. You're as silent as the wild creatures here. What do you want?'

'The skiing's finished, or at least, I've finished with it, so I just came out to make sure that you hadn't fallen or got lost. Why have you stayed behind?' He was careful not to mention Hugo's mishap, as agreed, so as not to worry her.

'For the same reason that the bear went over the mountain,' she stated bizarrely.

'I beg your pardon?' asked Beauchamp, totally uncomprehending.

'To see what he could see. That's why I'm not staying with the group. There's something out here; I'm convinced of it. I can't find anything amiss in the castle, although I haven't been down to the dungeons yet. That being the case, my nose tells me that there's something amiss on this estate, which was at the bottom of the piper's death.

'If it's not in the castle, then it's somewhere outside. I know how big the estate is, but if there's something iffy going on, it's not going to be going on too far away from the castle itself, otherwise there would be a lot of to-ing and fro-ing by Land Rover, and there hasn't been any evidence of that. It would also be inconvenient to have whatever it is secreted at a distance, when the weather's like this, and the winters in this region are long and hard.

'No, there's something within footfall of the castle, and I'm determined to hunt it out and find out what the dickens is going on here. One man's already lost his life. That needs avenging, if nothing else.'

'You could be putting yourself in grave danger, your ladyship. If whoever is behind whatever it is becomes aware of you sniffing around like a bloodhound; well, they've killed once, already. Do you think they'd hesitate to do it again?'

'It's very bad form to kill guests who are old friends of the family, Beauchamp.'

'The piper had been here all his working life, and he took over from his father before him, and they didn't hesitate to kill him. I think you're playing a very dangerous game, your ladyship. I shall do my very best to protect you, but even I have my limits.'

'That, I simply don't believe!' declared Lady A, in a slightly louder whisper.

'Hrmph!' Beauchamp cleared his throat in embarrassment at the level of confidence she had in him, then proposed something practical for the present. 'You wait here, and I'll slip off and tell the others that we're leaving the party, as you're having trouble with your arthritis, and we're just going to have a little walk before returning to sit in front of the fire.'

'Blasted cheek! I'm as fit as a fiddle!'

'It's what's known as a little white lie, your ladyship; then we can do exactly as you please, but I shall be by your side in case … anything happens.'

Lady Amanda unexpectedly gave in without a whimper, suddenly realising that 'anything' could happen out here in the wilds, too far away to summon help by her screams. 'Will do, old stick. I'll just hang around here in case that jolly old stag comes back for a gawp around.'

When Beauchamp returned, he found Lady Amanda on point, like a hunting dog who is pinpointing its prey. 'What's caught your attention, then, your ladyship?' he asked. She did not move an inch, merely muttering inconsequentially, 'I do wish you'd call me Amanda.'

'That is a request with which I am unable, at this present time, to comply. What has attracted your attention so strongly?'

'Look over there,' she said, pointing with her stick. Just between that tallest Douglas fir and the misshapen pine. It's quite difficult to distinguish with the sky so whitey-grey, but just keep looking.'

'For what, exactly, am I looking?' asked Beauchamp, with impeccable grammar.

'Little puffs of smoke – it may be steam, but I'm not a connoisseur of the difference between them at a distance. There goes one now!'

'I see what you mean. It's coming from quite a distance away. What do you suppose it is, your ladyship? If it were a bonfire, even at this distance, we'd smell it.'

'I have a fair idea, but I don't want to say anything until we've had a chance to explore.'

'That's a lot further away than you might think. You'd never make it on foot.'

'Then you'll have to do it, if I can come up with a reason for why you're not valeting for Hugo. Actually, I suppose that no one will really notice you're gone, if we don't say anything. If anyone asks about you, I'll say you've come down with a stomach bug that's very infectious, and you've put yourself in quarantine, as you don't want it to spread through the other staff like wildfire. How about that?'

'That will do nicely. Shall I go now, or tomorrow?'

'Go now. I'll make my way back to the castle, and if anyone asks me why I'm alone, I'll say that you've already returned because of illness, and make a huge fuss about how awful it was when your symptoms first appeared.

'If no one sees me, I'll go straight to your room, and make a loud fuss inside it, groaning on your part, and cajoling you to get to bed, on my behalf. Then, if anyone hears what's going on in your room, they'll assume that we're both in there. Give me your key, and I'll lock the door when I leave, so that no one can burst in and see that you're not there.

'When you get back, make straight for my room, and if anyone stops you, say it must have been one of those swift and ghastly bugs, but that you're feeling a lot better now, and were just going to report to me for duty, but make sure you get out of those warm clothes first, otherwise they'll know you haven't been back.'

'Neat!'

'Don't you dare go American on me! Now, off you toddle, and if you're not back by morning, I'll have to report you missing. Good luck, old bean! Happy hunting!'

'If I'm not back before morning, I'll be somewhere out here, dead of hypothermia.'

'If you get lost, there are bothies scattered all around for hunters to seek shelter. You'll never be far away from somewhere to make yourself comfortable, if you haven't got time to get back this evening.'

'Thank God for that! I had visions of you having to defrost me, so that I could make early morning tea. I don't really fancy turning into an icicle. And yes, before you ask, I do have a torch, and this little novelty,' he announced, producing a blackjack from his pocket. 'And if that's no good, I'll just have to use these,' he continued, taking some brass knuckles from another pocket.'

'Really, Beauchamp! That's disgraceful! I can't imagine why you thought you might need either of those, skiing. Well done! I'm not sure they didn't base James Bond on you.'

Lady Amanda, by using a side entrance and a different staircase, managed to sneak up to Beauchamp's room without being seen. It was to her advantage that the servants were all involved in preparing lunch, for although the stalkers had, in the end, been sent off with a picnic lunch, the guests who had gone off for a sleigh ride and the skiers would be coming back ravenous, after all that time spent in the cold, and would, no doubt, expect to be fed extravagantly, even though there was fat chance of that happening in this establishment.

She shot into her manservant's bedroom like a guilty mistress, closing the door firmly behind her, locking it, and mentally preparing her script, in anticipation of a fine theatrical time. She'd loved acting as a child, and had actually appeared in one of the Belchester Amateur Dramatic Society's productions. (They were known as the BADS, and for very good reasons other than their initials.)

With very mixed feelings, she got into the bed, making sure that her head made a good dent in the pillow, and wriggled around to make sure that the under-sheet was disturbed. Then she threw back the bedclothes and surveyed her handiwork. If anyone managed to get in here, they'd believe that Beauchamp was somewhere else, battling his bug.

She then pulled up an old oak chair that had been placed against the wall, and settled down to do her bit for the theatrical world. 'Groan, moan, pitiful sigh.' She produced these noises in her best contralto, sounding as male as she could, then switched pitches.

'You just lay there, Beauchamp. The bathroom's within easy reach, and there's a plastic bowl in there, should you need it. I've filled up your water container, and I'll pop up, hourly, to see how you are. Don't worry about your duties. Hugo and I can manage quite all right on our own for a short while.'

'Moooaan, slight pitiful wail of pain and despair. Grooooaan.' That sounded convincing enough, and she suddenly realised she felt like Ray Alan with her hand up an invisible Lord Charles. She even had her right hand in the air, as if operating a ventriloquist's dummy and, noticing this, thanked God that she didn't have her hand up the rear end of a green duck.

'Stay exactly where you are, and I'll bring you up a cup of tea later, and maybe some bread and butter. Now, just go to sleep and don't worry about anything else, except getting better,' she said in a raised voice, as she slipped out of the room and locked the door. That should do it, she thought, bustling out of the servants' quarters and making her way back to her own room to get changed for luncheon.

Finally making her way downstairs, she ran into the sleigh-ride party arriving back from their invigorating slither through the snow. Drew and Moira Ruthven, and Siobhan their hostess, were chattering happily about the beautiful snowscapes they had seen, and St John Bagehot could be seen making a determined line for the dining hall, oblivious of his erstwhile companions.

Lady Amanda made straight for the open fire in the drawing room and found Hugo entrenched in front of it, a hot toddy in his hand and a woollen blanket over his knees. Taking the chair on one side of the blazing logs, she asked Hugo how he had enjoyed his skiing lesson, and the unlikely sportsman burst into peals of laughter.

'I never realised I was an acrobat, but I did a fair impression of one, going down that slope. I was completely out of control, but it was terribly invigorating to realise the speed at which I was travelling, and the danger that that presented. Fortunately, I was well wrapped up and must have behaved rather like a rubber ball, for when I landed in a heap of ski poles and arms and legs at the bottom, I didn't seem to be any the worse for it. I only hope there's no bruising to come out.'

'You fell,' replied Lady A, acidly. 'Have you no consideration for anyone else, Hugo. What would I do without your company, now that I've become so accustomed to it? How selfish of you.'

'I'm fine, Manda, hic,' said Hugo, with the slightest of slurs, and Lady A immediately rang for a maid and ordered a pot of very strong coffee, as Mr Cholmondley-Crichton-Crump was a little tired and emotional. It was only his accident that had pried a healthy slug of alcohol out of Cook, but it seemed to have gone to his head beautifully.

'Really, Hugo. You're well on your way to being puddled. What sort of a detective are you? A lush?'

The stalking party arrived back just as the sun set and darkness descended. All were ruddy of face, their breath smoking like a huddle of dwellings, as they approached the entrance. All seemed to have had a good time, and disappeared straight upstairs to get ready for dinner at the extraordinarily early time it was served to guests of the McKinley-Mackintoshes.

Just before the dressing gong was sounded, there was a minor emergency, when Beauchamp appeared through the front door, glassy-eyed, blue with cold, and staggering. Walter Waule and Enid Tweedie had been crossing the hall carrying various accoutrements that would be needed during the meal, and rushed to his aid.

Taking an arm each, they led him to his room, half-carrying him. Not only was he unable to walk any further unaided, but he was incoherent as well, and they feared for his health. Surprised to find his room already locked, Walter produced a master key, and went straight to Beauchamp's bathroom to run a hot bath.

Enid helped him settle into a wing-backed chair and tutted about the state of his bed. It was not like Beauchamp to be lax about things like bed-making, and she was not party to Lady A's earlier theatrical performance. After this, she made herself scarce, while Walter undressed the semi-conscious manservant and helped him into the steaming water. This was none of her business.

Instead, she headed for the kitchen quarters, and informed everyone that Beauchamp was ill, and she needed at least two hot water bottles and a hot milky drink to help revive him. After being obliged, she took these back upstairs and tapped on the door nervously. She was a coy woman, and just the thought of catching Beauchamp 'in the buff' made her blush – although not completely with embarrassment, she was ashamed to find.

Walter let her in and explained that he had already got Beauchamp into bed. 'The water went cold almost immediately,' he informed her. 'His body just sucked all the heat out of it, and I took advantage of that to get him into his pyjamas and under the covers.'

Enid pulled back the covers bravely and placed one hot water bottle at his feet and one on his stomach, and put the cup of cocoa down on the bedside table. 'Try to drink it, please. I don't know what happened to you, but I'll come back after dinner with a pot of tea, and check on your condition,' she assured the still silent figure, whose arms had clutched at the hot water bottle at his middle like a drowning man clutching at a life-belt, and was now hugging it to himself like a teddy bear.

She pulled the covers back over his now recumbent body and tucked him in tightly, like a mother putting a sick child to bed, then left him in peace to sleep, Walter following her out of the room.

'Well, what did you make of that?' he asked.

'I haven't got the faintest idea, but I'll leave him to recover a bit before I start questioning,' replied Enid with a steely glint in her eye. This was Lady Amanda's doing, she was sure, and she did not approve at all.

'And, I'd be grateful if you kept it to yourself,' she exhorted Walter, who nodded his head in agreement, wondering if there were something wrong with the manservant that compelled him to wander off into the wide blue yonder.

Lady A was going to get the rough side of her tongue, Enid thought defensively, for whatever foolish errand she had sent the poor man on, and in this weather, too.

Chapter Six

Dinner held only one surprise. As they all trooped downstairs, a pipe was making a noise like a cat in a mangle in the main entrance hall, and each of them looked at the others, to see if anyone had any explanation for this unexpected replacement for Jock Macleod, but it was a complete mystery to all of them.

Their curiosity was satisfied, however, just before the serving of the first course, when Sir Cardew banged a spoon on the table and announced that they had taken on a young piper for a month's trial, and he was sure they'd all appreciate the presence of his music, not only for dancing at the wake for the previous holder of the post, before their unexpectedly prolonged stay was over, but as a reveille in the mornings. He didn't look very happy as he announced this.

Hugo groaned, and leaned towards Lady A to whisper, 'Not again! I had forgotten that there were two seven o'clocks in one day. I haven't had to cope with that since I did my stint in the army. At that hour, I haven't finished with the night, and would appreciate being left alone, to an hour that I consider to be the start of the day, and not at a time when I'm well away, and just getting my best quality sleep. And I'd completely forgotten that we were supposed to be having a wake for Macleod.'

'I'll slip you a pair of ear plugs, Hugo. Now do stop moaning. A wake won't hurt you, unless it's far too early in the morning,' replied Lady A acidly, quite exasperated with a Hugo who saw ghosts, did cartwheels down nursery slopes, and then got squiffy.

Conversation was all about their day's outings, the cold, the beauty, and the atmosphere in the ice-encrusted forest. As the meal ended, and the guests adjourned for 'coffee', Sir Cardew left them. He always smoked his daily post-prandial cigar outside at the base of the west tower.

Leaning contentedly against the stone wall, he looked out on the winter scene of clusters of light, and the great shadows of the forest and hills, black lumps weakly illuminated but unidentifiable in the dim light of the stars. The moon was new, and hiding modestly behind a cloud on this, her debut night.

Puffing contentedly on his cigar, appreciative of the rich, pungent smoke it produced, and which Siobhan hated so much, he was a happy man, with the exception of one fly in his metaphorical ointment, but he wouldn't allow himself to dwell on this. This was his daily dream-time. Sir Cardew looked deep into his mind and dreamt.

Sometime later, back in the drawing room, coffee was now over and a ghastly non-alcoholic liqueur was being served (these being kept separate in this household). Lady Siobhan gathered her guests close enough to listen, and asked them if they had ever seen the family broadsword. On receiving a uniformly negative answer, she offered to take them to view it in one of the south tower rooms, which was always kept locked, for it held a multitude of ancient and valuable family documents and Cardew did not consider a safe sufficient security. The locked room gave another layer of impenetrability that soothed his fears of burglary.

Everyone queued, in a very British way, at the cloakroom to get access to their outer garments, for many parts of the castle seemed colder than outside, then Siobhan led them off down corridors, round corners, and finally up a flight of narrow and very worn stone spiral steps that Hugo wouldn't even attempt to climb, waiting patiently at the foot, still glowing from the various points of the day in which he had imbibed alcoholic liquors.

Lady Amanda puffed and blew in the rear, determined to get her two-penn'orth, after all this cavorting through freezing corridors. The only thing she knew about broadswords was that they were very long and heavy, and it took a strong and fit man to wield one, and she was determined to see it.

She was thwarted, however, as soon as Siobhan opened the door to the strong room, which she referred to as the 'muniment room', she wailed in disbelief. The glass case in which the sword had been presented was smashed, and the sword had gone, taken, no doubt, by whoever had managed to get through the locked door to secure their prize, and then managing to relock the door, before departing with the filched weapon.

Disappointment was palpable in the air. They had made quite a trek to view this historical sword, and now it proved that their efforts had been all for nothing. A buzz of disappointment echoed round the chamber, joined by the faint voice of Hugo calling, 'Are you going to be much longer? It's brass-monkey weather down here.'

His plea had momentarily halted their chatter and, in the silence that followed there was a scream from outside, cut off almost as soon as it was audible.

'Whatever was that?' Lady Amanda was the first to ask. Another silence followed, in which Siobhan began to moan softly. 'Whatever's wrong, my dear? It's hardly something that can be put up for sale on the open market, and I'm sure it'll be recovered soon. If not, the insurance will take care of it.'

'It's not that,' she replied, her voice rising in panic. 'Cardew's outside. What if something dreadful has happened to him? I must go out and look for him.'

'Not on your own, you don't,' stated Lady A firmly.

'We'll all go. If he's fine, which I'm sure he is, we'll just say we're having a little starlight stroll, and then encourage him back inside, so that you can tell him about the theft.'

Collecting Hugo into their midst on the way down, they headed outside. Siobhan had explained to them Cardew's nightly ritual of smoking his only cigar of the day, so they all began to approach the west tower en masse. As they walked, slowly now, in case there really was something ghastly waiting for them, Lady A rummaged about in her handbag and produced a fair-sized torch.

Hugo glanced at her with amazement, but she merely replied, 'I just like to be prepared for all eventualities; that's all,' and quickened her step slightly, to catch up with the others, who were chattering about what might have happened. As they turned to go round the west tower, however, there was complete silence, and it was only Lady Amanda's out-of-breath question that broke this stunned silence. 'Anything afoot?' she puffed, as she arrived slightly tardily, then saw what they had already seen.

Sir Cardew was pinned to the ground, literally, the handle of the mighty broadsword sticking out of the top of his head, the point of the blade embedded in the grass between his feet, beside which his cigar slowly smouldered into extinction.

Another scream rent the air!

What to do? An out-of-hours call to Inspector Glenister threw up the fact that he would not be able to get a helicopter to the castle before daylight, having not long departed, and so it was decided, there would have to be a guard kept on Sir Cardew's cadaver overnight, so that foxes and the like wouldn't nibble at it. It would also have to be a guard comprised of two people, so that the murderer would have neither time nor opportunity to destroy any evidence left behind, due to there being a witness with him – or even her.

The sword must have been dropped: the thing was so heavy, Siobhan explained, that she couldn't even lift it. The west tower being the highest, just dropping it would prove fatal. Its own weight, aided by the process of falling, would easily slip through flesh and bone like a hot knife through butter, and the fact that it had actually pinned Cardew to the ground was put down more to luck than judgement, on the part of the murderer.

No one could have foreseen that incredible accuracy occurring. The original objective was evidently just to kill him. But why? And who? They already knew with what. There was absolutely no need to search for a weapon.

It was finally decided that the outdoor staff would be roused and rostered, in pairs, to be on guard throughout the night, and Macdonald was summoned to drag an ancient brazier out from some disreputable part of the nether regions of the castle, so that no one froze to death before morning. Moira took the weeping Siobhan back inside, and the others dispersed for the night. There was nothing more to be done until Glenister arrived on the morrow.

When Lady A and Hugo reached the comparative warmth of the entrance hall, they found Enid Tweedie standing at the bottom of the staircase wringing her hands, a look of great relief flooding her face, when she caught sight of the two friends.

'Thank God you're here,' she cried. 'I went to the drawing room after dinner and found no one there. I had no idea where you'd gone. It was like finding a land-locked Marie Celeste.'

'I thought there was someone missing at dinner. Have you been expelled from serving because you can't recognise a plate?' asked Lady A, facetiously, then softened her manner as Enid burst into sobs. This wasn't like her at all and, between gulps and sniffles, she explained that she'd been looking after 'poor Beauchamp'.

'Whatever's wrong with Beauchamp? As far as I know he's never had a day's illness in his life,' his half-sister said, speaking rather more softly.

'Robust chap, Beauchamp!' declared Hugo. 'Can't imagine the man ill.'

Edith explained how he had arrived back at the castle earlier, the parlous condition in which he'd arrived, and what Walter Waule and she had done to treat him. 'He was on the verge of hypothermia, you know. He couldn't walk or speak when we got him inside.

'Once he was sleeping, I excused myself from any other duties, as I am supposed to be your lady's maid, and I've been sitting by his bedside ever since. I only came down again because I looked out and saw a group of people heading for the front door, so I rushed down to see if you were amongst them.'

She had hardly finished speaking when Lady A went tearing up the stone stairs, two at a time, shouting, 'Beauchamp, Beauchamp, are you all right?' Enid and Hugo followed at a more sedate pace; one that suited Hugo's two still-unreplaced joints, and allowed Edith to recover her aplomb.

When they were all gathered together in the manservant's bedroom, Enid was absolutely dumbfounded to see Lady A throw one arm around Hugo and another around Beauchamp and burst into tears. This was a unique occasion, and she kept her silence in respect for this bombshell behaviour.

Lady Amanda's shoulder shook as she wailed, 'I nearly lost both of you in one day. Whatever would I have done? Life wouldn't have been worth living without the two of you. I sent you off, Hugo, on a fool's errand, to try skiing, and I sent you, Beauchamp, on what turned out almost to be a suicide mission. How can you ever forgive me?

'What a fool I am, never to consider the consequences

of my little whims, but you know what I'm like when I get the scent of blood in my nostrils. I'm like a stupid bloodhound: nose down, following, and damn what the rest of the world's doing.'

Hugo disentangled himself from her embrace: he found close contact with another, whoever it was, intensely uncomfortable, but patted her on the shoulder in an avuncular manner. Beauchamp also freed himself and commented, 'No harm done, er, Manda. How's the sleuthing coming along? I do have some news.'

Enid approached the bed and asked if he'd like a nice cup of tea – the panacea of the masses – thinking that the manservant even looked formally attired in his pyjamas. The jacket, which was the visible half, appeared to have been freshly ironed while he was wearing it and, although he was still a little wan-looking, he seemed none the worse for his experience.

'I'll bring a tray so we can all perk ourselves up, shall I?' she chirped, and made her way down to the kitchen. When she arrived there, there was a black cat curled up in front of the range, and the sight cheered her. A noise from the doorway alerted the animal. It took one look towards whoever was entering, fluffed up its fur in fear, and shot out of the room as if its tail were on fire.

Looking over her shoulder, Enid espied Sarah Fraser approaching the huge old fridge, and thought that the lump of a girl looked exactly like a Rottweiler in lipstick. It would be a brave man who took that on for a wife.

The lump of a girl looked at Enid and commented, 'That cat thinks he's Russian.'

Enid fell for it. 'Why's that?'

'Because anyone who sees him tells him to bugger off – Buggerov – get it?'

Enid merely sniffed, being very fond of cats herself, and had actually had one until quite recently.

Through the back door, Angus Hamilton the chauffeur,

who had just finished polishing the cars, came in rubbing his cold hands together and called out, 'Sarah, will ye make a wee cup o' tea for the two of us, and we can have a nice bitty chat?'

Sarah glanced briefly at him in/ disgust, and replied, 'Feck off, ye dirty owl man,' before stumping out of the kitchen in high dudgeon.

Enid shook her head, thinking that, with a face and figure like that, Sarah should take every chance she was offered. Hostility never produced any orange blossom, and that was a fact.

When she returned with the tea tray, Beauchamp had been apprised of the details of Sir Cardew's grisly fate, and was as flummoxed as the others as to who or why anyone would attempt something so macabre. 'We need to make some associations!' declared Lady A. 'There's something very improper,' (so typical of her to use a word like that) 'going on around here, and two people have died so far.

'We're actually in situ, and we have the best chance of sorting out the good guys from the bad. After all, this won't be the first time we've done it. I suggest we have a meeting in the morning, to pool all we can about who associates with whom, who might have been observed in a place they were unlikely to be found ... and all that jazz,' she concluded.

'And now, Enid, we have managed to suppress Beauchamp's eagerness to tell us of what he discovered on his ill-fated trip into the forest, so I suggest that, if we are all sitting comfortably, he begin.'

Beauchamp put down his cup on the bedside locker, cleared his throat, and launched into his story. 'Lady Amanda,' he began, a little embarrassed that that was the second time he had uttered her forename this evening, 'sent me off ... no, let me start at the absolute beginning.

'I had gone to the nursery slope with Mr Hugo, but the

skiing didn't last long after Mr Hugo's display of acrobatics. I decided that I would catch up with her ladyship, as the stalking group had left later than the skiing party, and eventually caught up with her on the edge of the forest.

'Something had caught her eye in the distance, and I was dispatched to investigate what was causing the thin spiral of white smoke that was rising in the distance. It was a lot further away than either of us had imagined, and it took me some considerable time to reach the source. And it seemed that the stalking party had wasted no time in taking advantage of you "bunking off", your ladyship.

'They were all there, outside this wooden construction, and it was from this that the thin spire of smoke was rising. Sir Cardew, Wriothesley (we call him Rizzly Grizzly in the servant's hall), Wallace Menzies – he's known as 'Mingin'', and Macdonald were all gathered together in a huddle. When they went inside, I got as close as I could, to see exactly what was going on inside the building, if I can dignify such a ramshackle structure as that, as such, and I managed to get a peek through one of the filthy panes of glass.

'They had a huge still going in there: a huge and completely illegal still, I might add. Well, I scarpered after that, and it was just as well I didn't' hang round, for the light was going, and I'm afraid I was led astray a few times. I never realised before how much one tree looks like another. It's all so much more difficult at twilight.

'Anyway, I think that answers a lot of our questions as to why. We need to work on the fine details, however. How on earth did the piper get involved in all this? Was he part of the 'gang', for want of a better word? Who took the sword? Was it a lone action, or part of a conspiracy? And why Sir Cardew? We still have a long way to go, with respect.'

'Oh, Beauchamp, it's so good to have you back on

form. When you didn't come back and there were no cocktails, I had the most enormous senior moment, for I thought you'd stayed on at the ski slope to perfect the art, knowing what you are for getting things exactly right. How can you forgive me for such laxity?'

'Precisely!' cut in Hugo. 'I had to make us a gin and tonic, and very poor it was too. I know it's only two ingredients, but it tasted foul, and had no kick whatsoever.'

'That's because I usually mix two parts gin to one part tonic,' Beauchamp informed him, with a knowing smirk.

Things were back to normal. For now.

The day, with all its unfamiliar activities, was followed by an equally disturbing night. Lady A and Hugo had had a brandy in front of the former's fire before turning in, leaving Enid to pander to Beauchamp's every whim, and didn't get to bed until well after the witching hour, Lady A completely forgetting to furnish her friend with earplugs in defiance of the, now forgotten, new morning piper.

Her ladyship went out like a light, to use a rather vulgar expression, but Hugo tossed and turned, regularly discovering new parts of his body that seemed to be developing what felt like spectacular bruises. He managed to doze for a while, then dreamt that he was tied up and being terrorised by some terrible brute.

When he awoke, in a muck-sweat, he found himself so tangled in the sheets that he could barely move a muscle, and spent some time undoing the knot that he had made of himself and the bedding, huffing and puffing and muttering, 'Damn!' 'Blast!' and 'Tiddlywinks!' under his breath, as his over-exercised muscles protested at such brutal treatment.

Eventually getting himself settled again, although he had had to get out and remake the bed, he tried once more to go to sleep, but such a benison eluded him still, and it wasn't until two-thirty that he finally slipped into a light doze. What seemed like only a minute or two later, but was in fact over an hour, he became aware of something in close proximity to his head, opened his eyes, and found himself staring into the same dark-veiled countenance as he had, on one previous occasion.

When Hugo screamed, it was in a surprising falsetto pitch, and this noise pierced Lady Amanda's deep sleep of the innocent. Realising immediately that the noise was coming from Hugo's room, she leapt from her bed, ready for action, grabbed a poker from beside the fireplace, and shot through the adjoining door – or, at least, that's what she had intended to do.

She, herself, in an inattentive moment, had slipped the bolt on her side when Hugo had left her for the night, and she merely rebounded from its solid surface and landed in a heap on the floor, the poker committing an act of gross indecency upon her person. As she rose to hands and knees, she could hear shouting from the adjoining room. 'Manda! Manda! Are you being attacked? Someone's locked the door? Who's in there with you?'

Slowly she rose to her feet and slipped the bolt, and the door shot open from the other side. This was unfortunate, as it opened into her room, and she went down with the poker again with a not surprising feeling of déjà vu. 'Manda! Manda! What's happening in there?' bellowed Hugo, just making things worse by pushing the door and shoving her further across the floor.

'Oh, there you are,' he said, espying her prone figure. 'I thought the door was unconscionably heavy. Are you all right? What's been going on in here? It sounded like you were being murdered.'

'I merely reacted to your screaming,' she declared, with as much dignity as she could muster, being helped from the floor in her nightshirt by Hugo's gallant efforts.

'But what was all that banging and bumping I heard?'

he enquired, not understanding why there had been such a rumpus from the adjoining room, and why his friend was holding a brass poker in such a threatening manner. 'Don't hit me, please.'

Lady A returned the poker to its usual position, sat down in a fireside chair, and indicated Hugo to follow her lead and take a seat. 'I heard your screams, grabbed the poker in case you were in mortal peril, then threw myself at the adjoining door to come to your rescue. Unfortunately, I must have unthinkingly slipped the bolt when you went to bed – boing-ed off the dratted thing like a ricocheting missile, and then got into a terrible tangle with my nightshirt and the poker. That's all.

'Then you barged in and pushed me along as if I were a mop with which you were washing the floor. Just look at the state of my nightshirt! Really, these flagstones are a disgrace. I shall complain to housekeeping in the morning. Someone is being lax in their duties in this establishment, and I will not stand for it; even if I do know how a mop feels, being pushed around with no will of its own.

'So, why were you making all that fuss in the first place? The noise was enough to waken the dead.'

'I think it actually did, Manda. I had a terrible time trying to get off. The first time I dozed off, I woke, practically mummified in the sheets, then, when I'd sorted that out and remade the bed, I managed, at last, to go to sleep. But it wasn't for long.

'I felt something vile hovering over me, and when I opened my eyes, there she was again – that awful woman with the black veil, and I just started to wail like a banshee. Honestly, I couldn't help myself. Then, of course, I heard noises that I thought were you being attacked, and it seemed like someone had sussed what we were up to, and was determined to wipe out both of us, before we found out any more. Shall I pour us a brandy to settle our nerves?'

'I should think so!' agreed Lady A vehemently, as she slid into a dressing gown, modesty insisting that she should not be in a bedchamber in the presence of a man – even if it was only Hugo – dressed in just her nightgown.

They had barely settled to sip their nightcap that was nearly a 'morning-cap' when there were noises from beyond the window. It sounded exactly like the jingling of bottles on a milk float, but no milk float would come out to this isolated dwelling.

As Hugo rose to investigate, Lady Amanda grabbed him by the tail of his nightshirt and insisted, 'No, Hugo! Not with the lights on! Let's turn them out, then we can peek through the curtains, and they won't know that we're watching, whatever is going on out there.'

Hugo realised the logic of this, and extinguished the lights, before they approached the draughty regions of the window. There was a low whistle as the wind entered through the ill-fitting frame, and made the room several feet away from it as icy as right next to it.

The castle being situated so far north, there was already a dim light in the sky; certainly enough for them to distinguish what was going on down below on the frontage. There might not be a milk float down there, but there was some sort of cart, filled with boxes that rattled and jingled every time one of them was lifted from its rear. Just beyond the intimidating entrance doors, a small door had been opened in the wall, and men could be seen transporting said boxes through this door, and disappearing slowly into the ground.

'It must be an entrance to the cellars-cum-dungeons,' Lady Amanda breathed in Hugo's ear, then added, 'and I don't think that's milk they're delivering, either. That's a hooch float we can see down there. They're transferring what they have manufactured in the hut that Beauchamp discovered, and they're making sure that nothing is discovered there, when the police return. They're stashing it in the cellar, and I bet there's some sort of concealed entrance down there where they think they can stash it, undetected.'

'What shall we do?' Hugo breathed into her ear, tickling her with his night-time wayward mop of white hair. Such close proximity between them had not prevailed since they had danced together in times that seemed a lifetime away, and they both slipped apart, ending up at opposite ends of the window, without a word being said.

'Meeting, tomorrow morning,' hissed Lady A, 'and not a word of this to Glenister. I don't want him plodding his size fourteens all over the place, and giving the game away that someone's on to them.'

'What about my ghost?' asked Hugo, peeved that his experience had been relegated to the bottom of the division, in the light of this new occurrence.

'Indigestion!' was the only reply he got, before Lady A stumped over to her bed, slipped off her dressing gown, and got in, pulling the covers over her. 'Draw the curtains when you leave, Hugo. I don't want to see you again until the morning. And if you get any other visits from wandering females, kindly instruct them to get a mop and bucket and do something about these filthy flagstones and at least be of some use, instead of just frightening the bejeezus out of you, and disturbing my rest.'

Chapter Seven

The auspices for the next morning were not good, with so much sleep lost, and then the unwelcome serenade by the new piper, who excelled himself, and made a noise like half a dozen cats caught in a giant bicycle, but Beauchamp came up trumps, as usual.

Although he did not know of their wee small hours disturbances, he wanted to show his appreciation for the care and concern he had been shown the day before, after his awful experience in the snowy forest, and had raided the kitchen to the tune of one frying pan, a stick of lard, four eggs, numerous rashers of bacon, two tomatoes, and a hunk of uncut bread.

These he transported into the little room beside Lady A's room, from which he produced cocktails and afternoon tea, and treated them to breakfast in bed, which went a considerable way to reining in their grumpy moods, and getting them off to a good start to the day. Above all, it was such a treat to get tea that tasted of something other than dishwater.

He had actually been heard singing, as he prepared the food, and Lady A immediately identified the song as a very old one: 'If I were the only boy in the world ...' warbled tunefully into her room, startling her beyond comprehension. She had never known Beauchamp to sing, as long as she had known him, and that seemed to have been forever.

When she ran into Enid, she found out that the police had already arrived, along with a team of photographers and evidence gatherers, and that the giant human kebab had been removed from public view. That was a relief. She still could not get out of her mind the vision of the poor man speared through like a pig ready for the fire pit. Even the adventures of the night before had not wiped it out, and it had haunted her dreams during what little sleep she had managed to get.

'… and I couldn't help but laugh afterwards. It was so incongruous,' she heard Enid conclude, and had to apologise.

'I'm sorry, Enid, but I was miles away, wondering what Siobhan will do now. Of course, this is her ancestral home, so I suppose she'll just try to keep things going the way she always remembered them. After all, the castle has come down through her family and not Cardew's.'

'I was just telling you how unlikely it was to see Beauchamp in a bobble hat, yesterday. I've only ever seen him in his chauffeur's cap or his 'going into Belchester' bowler. If he hadn't been in such a bad way when he got back here, I don't think I could have stopped myself from laughing."

'Good grief! I was so taken up with what I had just seen and wanted investigated, that I didn't even notice. We must get him to put it on again, so I can enjoy the experience thoroughly. What colour was it?' she asked, inconsequentially.

'Blue and white, with a little red in the bobble,' replied Enid, who would never forget the sight.

'That's Beauchamp – patriotic as ever.'

Their conversation was interrupted at that moment, as Evelyn Awlle came squawking down the main staircase, her hands in the air, and a look of total despair on her face. 'Whatever's the matter, Evelyn? You look in a rare old state,' asked Lady Amanda.

'It's the mistress, your ladyship. I left her a little late this morning after what happened yesterday an' all, but when I took some tea up to her room, she wasnae there, and her bed had nae been slept in. I don't have any idea what could have happened to her, but I'm afraid for her life, after what happened to the master yesterday.'

Others, having heard the cries of distress of Siobhan's lady's maid, were gathering in the hall at the foot of the stairs to see what was occurring, and Lady A immediately took charge of things. 'Can someone get Inspector Glenister? It would seem that Siobhan has disappeared, maybe as long ago as last night, and poor Evelyn here is concerned for her safety.

'Now, it could just be that she used another room, as she was so upset at what had happened to Cardew. That has to be checked out first, so if someone would kindly fetch the inspector, he can organise a search of the castle, before we cast our worries any further afield.'

By the time Glenister arrived, it seemed that the whole of the household had assembled in the great entrance hall, staff included, and it didn't take long to explain to him what the problem was. He rounded up his men, and they were allocated different floors and wings to search.

He then took Lady A to one side and, with an ironic smile, informed her that he hoped that none of her belongings would be found in connection with this most recent body. 'Otherwise it would have rather a damning implication for yourself, would it not, your ladyship?'

She gave him a very old-fashioned look, then gathered together Hugo, Enid and Beauchamp, and led them off to the library, where they could talk in privacy. She and Hugo possessed information that the police did not, and she was determined that they would form a plan to uncover all the nefarious doings, before anyone else was hurt.

It would not only be quicker that way, bureaucracy being what it was, it would also be more fun. She had read rather more Enid Blyton and Agatha Christie books than were good for her in the past, and sometimes she forgot that she was as mortal as Jock Macleod and Sir Cardew had been.

'We have to find some way into where they keep the hooch,' declared Lady Amanda. 'We can't just approach it boldly from the front, as they did last night. We'd be seen immediately. We either find out where there is a key to the inside door and use that, or wait until tonight, and try to get in from the outside, when everyone else is asleep. Enid, it is getting imperative, in this career of sleuthing that we seem to be adopting, that you devote your spare time to knitting us some black or navy-blue balaclava helmets for future use.'

'I'll ask my mother, but I don't really have the time to produce four such pieces of headgear at the moment. I do have a life, you know?' declared Enid more boldly than she had ever addressed Lady Amanda before, and she didn't even blush.

'I should be most grateful if your mother would oblige. I shall provide everything she needs, plus remuneration for her time, when they are knitted. Thank you, Enid. We shall convene again in my room at nine o'clock tonight, if none of us is successful in locating a key. If, of course, we get our hands on one sooner, I shall round you all up for a little exploration. You and Enid start in the servants' quarters, Beauchamp, and Hugo and I will try a little desk and bureau exploration.'

Everyone assented to this plan, and they went their separate ways for now, Enid quietly crooning, 'The boy I love is up in the gallery ...' Goodness! She and Beauchamp both seemed to be steeped in old music hall songs at the moment, thought Lady A, and wondered whether something about this visit had brought that on.

Lady Amanda began her search with the big visitors' book that everyone had signed on arrival, and which was lodged overtly on the big hall table, so that anyone who cared to could have a peek through the names, to see illustrious visitors from the past. It was a prodigious volume going back several decades, rather like a burials register, she thought.

Heaving back the heavy pages, she certainly saw recognisable names from the political world of the past, along with a few raves from the showbiz grave, when Siobhan's parents had moved in higher circles than their daughter did today. But this wasn't getting the baby bathed, so she turned, rather reluctantly, back to the present and considered the entries made by her fellow guests, making a note of the addresses they had given. For some reason, this action seemed important, and she always followed her instincts.

Hugo had merely hung around while she did this, and when she questioned his inaction, he declared that he'd never been to the castle before, and had no idea of the layout, so he'd have to tag along with her, and let her direct his searching.

'I know there'll be no chance of getting into Cardew's study, because that's where Inspector Glenister will set up his lair, as before. I suggest we go in search of keys. We've just got to be careful whom we ask. There are a couple here whom I think are rather dodgy, but I do have a plan.

'I suggest that we ask to borrow the key to that tower room where we were shown that terrible broadsword. In the past, I've heard Mama refer to that as the muniment room, as Siobhan did when we discovered the sword was missing. If we can get in there, there should be a lot to sift through. Probably in all those chests that are around the walls. There may even be a key to that cellar door, whether it be inside or out. It's the sort of thing that might be kept there, locked away, so that there wouldn't be any unnecessary shenanigans with the staff. Old habits die hard.'

'But Manda, I couldn't get up those stairs last time I

tried, and I certainly haven't got any fitter since then. In fact, I'm covered in bruises, and ache from head to toe from that blasted skiing fiasco. You really are too trying! You'll have to do it on your own, or get Beauchamp or Enid to help you.'

'I'll go and see if I can find Enid. She's supposed to be my lady's maid, so I shall say I need her to do some 'maiding', right now.'

She found Enid taking her morning coffee with the other staff, and announced that she had need of her services. Draining her cup, Enid scuttled after her, bursting with curiosity. 'What are we going to do?' she asked, excitedly. 'Are we on the hunt?'

'We most definitely are, Enid. Oh, damn, I forgot to ask.'

'Ask what?'

Sliding back into the kitchen, Lady Amanda put on her most appealing smile (fairly frightening to those who did not know her well) and asked if she could have the key to the room where they had intended to view the sword even as it was being put to such dastardly use. 'Siobhan said I could borrow it for a few hours, but I didn't like to disturb her, this morning of all morning, and then I found out she had gone missing, so I've come here instead.' she leered at them. 'Just for a little research I'm doing, you know?'

There was no question; she was a guest, and they were staff. Cook handed over the large key without a murmur, dismissing the request as just another loony passion of one of the weird guests who sometimes stayed.

Having gathered her gang together, Lady Amanda explained what she had done so far, and suggested that they go, forthwith, to said muniment room to see what they could dig up. She hadn't wanted to chance asking outright for the key to either of the cellar doors, as someone might have been alerted to their intentions, but she felt confident that they would find a copy of at least one of the keys in their target room. And who knew what documents they might come across, perhaps ones referring to nefarious doings hidden from all eyes up there, for who was likely to want to go into such a dead room, were they not being shown the sword?

Hugo had suggested that he go into the library and start shaking out books, as he was too infirm to reach the muniment room, and Beauchamp said he had a little errand to run before he joined them. That left just Enid and Lady A, puffing up the stone corkscrew, grasping for dear life at the rope that represented a handrail, and squeaking slightly as they met particularly worn steps.

It took them so long to get up there that they were still staring at all the old trunks that needed searching, when Beauchamp bounded into the room behind them, a beaming smile on his face – a most unusual occurrence, as he, by nature, wore a poker face, both on and off duty. 'That didn't take long, Beauchamp. Any luck?'

'More than you could imagine, your ladyship. I betook myself to the cellar entrance, and the key was actually in the door. It seemed the obvious place to look – handy for anyone engaged in nefarious activities, and perfectly natural for anyone innocent. Why should the key not be in the door? It's not as if there would be a fortune in fine wines down there, now is it? This is, after all, a dry house, and the most one could expect would be a few bottles of whisky for future Burns' Nights.

'There's only a short flight of stairs down, for it's low-ceilinged down there. Anyway, inside the first cellar, just behind the door and not in one's sightline, were one just taking a peek inside, were three other keys. One was labelled for 'outer cellar', and another, 'exterior door'. There are, in fact, two chambers on that side of the castle. The third key was just labelled 'dungeons', and of the location of those, I am afraid I know nothing, as they

125

certainly don't lead off from the cellars. I took the lot!'

'Beauchamp, you are worth your weight in rubies. What was in there?' declared Lady Amanda, still a little out of breath from her climb up to the muniment room. Now, she decided, they might as well go back down. The keys were the main objective, and they could spend a fortnight up here, easily, going through the trunks. She believed that, with possession of the keys, and the addresses she had copied down from the visitors' book, they had something to work on.

Beauchamp replied in a rather frivolous manner. 'I shall not disclose the contents. I think it would be more fitting if we all went there together and took a look, and I suggest we leave that until rather later, so as not to arouse anyone's suspicions. It might be injurious to our hostess, should she have had the misfortune to have been kidnapped, although I assume she must be in the dungeons themselves, as I didn't come across her on my little fact-finding mission.'

Halfway back down to the ground floor, Lady Amanda bade the other two go on ahead. She was absolutely knackered, although she would never use that word aloud. She'd 'snail' her way down to Hugo to see if he'd dislodged anything interesting from the library books. As she plodded doggedly on, she wondered about Enid.

She had changed enormously since Hugo's arrival, and the events that had followed on from that. The woman was always in and out of hospital with some minor complaint like in-growing nose-hairs and septic toe (Lady A was not the most sympathetic of creatures) but now she had, it seemed, a new lease of life – and health.

She must just have been bored before, she decided, and seeking attention in the only way she knew how. She had, after all, had her demanding old mother living with her and a smelly old cat that did nothing but destroy things and leave intentional messes, although she was fond of both.

Hugo had, of course, found nothing. She had only given him the task because she didn't want him feeling left out, and eventually they all came together again in Lady A's room. Beauchamp having produced refreshments, Lady Amanda informed them of what she had gleaned from the visitors' book, and declared that they now needed a map. Those addresses were important in some way: she could feel it in her water. Hugo winced as she said this, and turned his head away at the very thought of Lady A's personal eau, wrinkling his nose in disgust. There were limits!

'No need for cumbersome old maps, your ladyship,' Beauchamp announced, 'for I have one of those electronic tablets that give one access to the internet and global maps, with zoom capabilities.'

'I have no idea at all what you're talking about, but I'm sure it's marvellous. Perhaps you would explain it to us?' Lady A wasn't very up on the latest technology, although she had a laptop, and a mobile phone, albeit a very ordinary model.

The manservant went to his half-sister's wardrobe and reached to the highest shelf. 'I left it in here for security,' he explained, bringing out a relatively small, flat, black plastic thing. 'This is the tablet,' he explained, 'and it works just like a computer, with a few other functions that are rather unique. I can log on to a global map site, type in the location of the addresses, and it should bring up a picture of that area. We can then zoom in for quite a close look, although it might get a bit fuzzy if we try to look too closely.'

'Whatever will they think of next?' exclaimed Lady A. 'I want one as soon as we get back home.'

'I can also search their names. If they're listed, we might learn a few interesting things from that service,' he continued.

'Actually, I want one NOW!' Lady Amanda had never

been known for her patience.

The only addresses that were actually in Scotland were those of Wallace Menzies and Quinton Wriothesley, although both men had excruciatingly posh English accents due to being sent away to school.

Menzies lived furthest north, on the coast, and it was possible to see what looked like a fishing business on the coast that was part of his land. Although Wriothesley lived further inland, a quick look for him on the internet revealed that he had a small haulage business. These two facts were very encouraging when allied with the other information they had gleaned.

Their meeting was interrupted, at that point in the proceedings, by Evelyn Awlle, who announced that Inspector Glenister had requested the presence of Lady Amanda in Sir Cardew's study, and he awaited her even as she spoke. Muttering under her breath, 'Bum! More dashed stairs,' Lady A rose, grabbed one of Hugo's walking sticks, and followed her from the room. Much more of this castle-exploring and she'd be after his walking frame when they got home.

Inspector Glenister greeted her with a hearty handshake and a smile. After requesting that she take a seat, he said, somewhat facetiously, 'No article belonging to you was found in connection with the corpse this time, so it would seem that I can eliminate you as our prime suspect for the piper's murder, and that of Sir Cardew.

'It appears, though, that someone is planning to go into the kebab business. What an extraordinary way to go about a murder. Do you have any idea about what's going on?'

Not wishing to lie, she decided to prevaricate. 'I can't imagine what could link the death of a piper with the death of our host,' and in a way, this was completely true. She didn't have a clue what linked these murders, but she was damned sure that they had something to do with the illegal hooch business that was being carried out on the estate, but hunches were not fact, so she felt quite justified in keeping her silence.

'I understand that no one was present – save for the murderer – when Sir Cardew was done away with. Can you confirm that?'

'I think we had all been taking some filthy non-alcoholic substitute for brandy in the library, but I can't be sure. They're such big rooms, and people were coming and going, and talking in pairs and groups that constantly reformed.'

'Come on, lassie! There were hardly hundreds of guests there,' the inspector declared, with a modicum of impatience.

'No, there weren't,' she retorted in a challenging voice, 'but then, no one told us we were going to have to make a statement about who talked to whom, who went off to the lavatory or to tidy their hair or make-up, and who may have gone to their room for something. We had no idea that we were to be held to account because there was going to be a murder. None of us has a crystal ball, you know!'

'I'm sorry if I sounded a little testy. It's just that I cannae seem to get an accurate picture of who was where, when the fatality occurred. And to top it all, we have Lady Siobhan's disappearance, and we don't know whether she's run away in distress, or whether she's been kidnapped, which seems vera unlikely, but we have to consider every avenue of possibility.'

As he finished his speech, there was a sharp rap on the door, and Constable MacDuff burst into the room waving a piece of paper in a gloved hand. 'There's a note, sir. It was nailed to the outside of the front door. I went outside for a wee toke on ma pipe, and there it was. It's a ransom note!' He was very excited, not just at the turn of events, but that he had been the one to find the note. The length of his rolled 'r's had increased with the progression of his triumphant tale of discovery.

'That confirms it, then,' declared Glenister. 'It is kidnapped, she's been. I'll need to get a search party together to go through the estate with a fingertip search. Do we know how many bothies and shelters there are in the forest? No doubt there are dozens, and the trees are vera dense in some parts. Have the evidence lads left yet? No? Right, well tell them to stay on, and procure as many members of the outside staff as you can. They know the estate better than anyone else, and their knowledge could prove invaluable.'

The constable bustled off full of self-importance, and Glenister once more turned his attention to his interviewee. 'I'm sorry, lassie, but this is of prime importance, now we know that Lady Siobhan has been taken against her will.'

'No problem, Inspector. I quite understand. And don't forget to pass on my best wishes to Adrian, when you speak to him next.'

'Ma wee Sassenach nephew? Aye, of course I will. I don't know if I've mentioned it before, but ma brother's no better than all these nobs who were born in this glorious country and whose parents sent them to posh schools and universities south of the border. Ma aen brother didnae want any children of his to speak with a Scottish accent, snob that he was. I must be off, but I'll need to speak to the rest of your party before I go, so don't leave the castle grounds, now will ye?' He seemed to have suddenly become more Scottish with the excitement, and begun to repeat himself in his agitation. 'And I'd better summon a hostage negotiator too,' he concluded.

Lady Amanda knew that his request not to leave the grounds was an order and not a polite request, and left him to it, as he was obviously eager to get on with the search for their hostess. She'd hobble her way back to the others, so that they could make plans. They certainly knew a lot of things. Now all they had to do was to put them together in a coherent story, and make plans for how to uncover all the dastardly deeds that were being committed on this estate.

Hugo was in the drawing room reading an old edition of *The Scotsman* which he had found lying around, and was apparently absorbed in it. Of Beauchamp and Enid, there was no sign. 'Hey-ho, old thing,' Lady Amanda greeted him wearily. Where are the other two?'

'Well, they were with me, but then Iain Smellie joined them, and informed them that Elspeth's maid had been doing a bit of eavesdropping, and had heard talk of some illegal goods being stashed somewhere. Anyway, the maid told Elspeth, Elspeth told Iain, and he went to Sir Cardew with the information. This was just before dinner last night. Iain said 'I don't know if it means anything with regard to what happened later, but I think we'd better inform the inspector, don't you?'

'I said he ought to do what he felt was right, and left it at that, and he scuttled off. Immediately, the other two took off for the staff quarters, to see if they could get anything more detailed from that Campbell girl, and then you arrived.'

'Good!' declared Lady Amanda, her spirits lifting. 'He won't find the inspector because he's getting a search party together. That constable – what was his name? MacDuff? – found a note nailed to the outside of the front door. I didn't get a good look at it, but they said it was a ransom note, so we know more than anyone else, at the moment.

'He won't have time to interview him, but he might get him to round up the other guests to help in the search party. I certainly hope so, because that'll give us the castle more or less to ourselves. We can plead age and infirmity, Hugo. Don't look at me like that! It's true! And we can plead that we need Beauchamp and Enid to help us. That should give us enough time to get together, assemble this new information, and come up with a plan.'

'You're using one of my walking sticks. You might have asked,' Hugo exclaimed, having just noticed it.

'See, I am infirm!' she declared, trumping his ace.

Now all they had to do was wait for the return of Beauchamp and Enid, to see what they had managed to winkle out of the dazzlingly ugly Mary Campbell.

When Beauchamp and Enid returned to the drawing room, they were bursting with news, the first item being more of culinary importance, than of interest in their investigations. 'We are charged with fending for ourselves until an early supper is laid out. It will be a cold collation for those returning from the search, to be self-served, as and when they return. May I offer you some smoked salmon sandwiches for your midday sustenance?'

'Butties be damned!' burst out Lady A, while Hugo murmured,

'That would be very nice, and good of you to suggest it, Beauchamp. Thank you.'

'Come on, man! Give! What did you find out? I'm bursting to know.'

Beauchamp gave them both a sweeping glance, and bowed his head slightly at Hugo, to affirm his appreciation of his good manners. 'It transpired that when the constable went to the staff quarters to ask for volunteers for the search party, he told them what was in the ransom note.'

Lady A and Hugo both sat forward in their seats eagerly, waiting for him to continue with the details. 'It appears that the note was written in disguised capital letters, and asked for safe passage for three, from the country, before they would return their hostage. If this was not complied with, they would kill her. The note was found nailed to the front door.'

'What lousy pen-pals they'd make,' was Lady A's comment on this last. 'Well, we know who two of those

132

three are already. One member of the little gang has been eliminated, and it's obvious that Siobhan knew nothing about any of the monkey business going on right under her nose. We need to foil those three, whoever the third member is – probably one of the woodsmen – and rescue Siobhan, before we can let any of what we know out.'

'Precisely,' agreed Hugo. 'Who'd believe us, with all these people of seemingly impeccable reputations under this roof? And if we say anything and let them know what we know, then they'll realise we know, and make a run for it before they can be taken into custody, don't you know?'

'Pardon?' asked Enid, confused with who knew what about whom, and what the result would be.

'Ignore him, Enid. He gets a bit like that sometimes. I don't know whether they're senior moments, or whether he's somehow related to Winnie the Pooh,' Lady A reassured her. 'The important thing now, is to decide what to do, and when to do it.'

'Well, whatever it is, I suggest we carry it out under cover of darkness, when everyone is safely asleep. We don't want to put poor Lady Siobhan in any more danger than she is in already,' declared Beauchamp, with impeccable logic, as usual. 'I'll get those sandwiches now, while Enid rustles up a nice pot of tea, then I suggest you two have a nap this afternoon, because it could be a very busy night for all of us.'

Chapter Eight

It was a very dark place, the only light filtering in from a tiny piercing of the wall, and Siobhan had no idea where she was, what time it was, or even if it was a different day. All she knew was that her ankles were in irons, as were her wrists. She could not stand, but could manipulate food and drinks.

These had been brought to her twice since she had been seized by someone wearing a dark ski mask, but she had no idea whether it was someone from the castle, or a complete stranger, seeing an opportunity she didn't understand.

She was lucky she had been wearing her dressing gown when she was taken, for it was cold here, wherever here was, and she'd had no idea that there had been a set of stone steps inside the walls of the castle. She thought she was in the dungeons, but she couldn't be sure, because a handkerchief soaked in something sweet and disgusting had been put over her face once the perilous staircase had been descended. In reality, she could have been transported anywhere. She had no way of knowing.

The food was delivered by the masked man, but she couldn't be sure whether it was the same one who had kidnapped her, or an accomplice. All she knew was that he didn't utter a word, so she had no way of identifying him from his voice.

Whoever it was had some sense of decency. There was an old china commode within her reach, and a roll of necessary paper, and this object had been emptied and returned on both occasions when she had been brought sustenance, so her captor couldn't be an out-and-out monster. She just wished it was either a little warmer here, or that they would bring her a blanket.

Her mind was in a turmoil about everything that had happened. It had started with the murder of their beloved family piper. Then Cardew had been brutally murdered, and here she was, kidnapped. Whatever she could have done to deserve all this, she had no idea. She hadn't thought that anyone hated her enough to deprive her of a member of staff, a husband whom she had grown rather used to over the years, and then her own liberty. She wondered how long it would be before she regained her freedom, if she were that lucky.

Then the terrible and terrifying reality struck her. What if she were never released, and spent the rest of her life in captivity – like the Man in the Iron Mask? Only without the mask! What if they killed her because they couldn't get whatever it was they wanted? If they (whoever 'they' were) would only ask, she'd give them anything she had, to get out of her current situation.

She was far too young to die, despite having reached what other people might consider a reasonable age. She simply wasn't ready. There were far too many things that she had never done, too many places that she had never seen. She wasn't ready for the castle to be handed down to the next generation. Was anyone even looking for her, or had they assumed that she had decided to go away for a few days, after the shock of the tragedy that had befallen her husband?

A thousand fears beset her racing mind, as she heard someone approaching the place where she was being held prisoner. Would this be food? Or was it Death, who came for her this time?

'If the ransom note was found nailed to the front door,' Lady Amanda was expounding, 'then why did no one hear it being done, and investigate. And surely someone would have seen them.'

'Because the note was merely speared on an extant nail, that has probably been there for decades,' said Beauchamp's distinctive voice just by her ear, and she shrieked with shock.

'How the heck did you get there? Oh, don't tell me. You have a tread with the lightness of a cat's,' she scolded her manservant, then, as he approached the coffee table in front of them, she saw his face, and her spirits soared. His expression was one of suppressed glee, and there was news in his eyes. 'You've got information, haven't you, Beauchamp? What is it? Was it that Campbell girl?'

'All in good time, your ladyship,' he advised, maddeningly, and proceeded to pour the tea for four, Enid joining them from behind his rather larger frame.

'Come on, man! You know you've got us in suspense.' Even Enid looked excited, and a little triumphant, knowing something that Lady A and Hugo did not.

When they were all seated, it not making any difference if guests and staff sat together, with the absence of almost all the usual characters who might disapprove, he told them what he had discovered. 'I didn't get any more from the Campbell girl ...'

Here, Enid interrupted him with a comment that was extremely un-Enid-like. 'When they handed out "pretty" she must have thought they said "shitty" and said she didn't want any. I've never seen anyone who looked so like a medieval gargoyle in my life.'

'Enid!'

'I'm perfectly entitled to have my own opinion, and state it,' she replied rebelliously, not at all like the meek little thing she had been until recently.

Beauchamp noisily cleared his throat. He was supposed to be the centre of attention, and he wasn't ceding that position to anyone, not even not-so-meek-mannered Enid.

'She couldn't actually identify the voices she heard, because she had her ear pressed to a door. She only knows that they were male voices, and the situation frightened her.'

There was a double sigh from his employer and her friend, and he quickly put them out of their misery, that he had found out something of worth. 'BUT,' he said, in capital letters, 'I was in the scullery looking for a tea-strainer – I don't know where they get to in this household. I think something must eat them. Anyway, while I was in that dismal cave of a room, I tripped over something: something that the old rag rug in there must have covered previously.' He stopped at that point, and smiled like the Cheshire Cat, teasing them with his reticence to finish the story.

'Go on, you rotter. You know how you've got us on tenterhooks.' Lady Amanda was losing her patience, and was getting ready to cuff her manservant round the ears, even if, or probably because, he had turned out to be her half-brother.

'It was an inset ring that hadn't been seated properly in its groove. There was no one around. Cook had gone off for her afternoon nap, Sarah Fraser had some mending and ironing to do for Mrs Elspeth, and Mary Campbell sloped off to have a soak in the bath with scented candles. Oh, the temptation to push such an ugly woman under the water and hold her there, thus putting her out of our misery, and yes; I did mean to say that.'

'Come on, Beauchamp, before I play the big sister with you. And stop being so cruel about the poor girl. She can't help the way she was born.'

Beauchamp actually chuckled, then went on, 'I pulled it up, having pushed the scullery door shut, and found that it led to a flight of stone steps. I feel certain I have discovered the entrance to the dungeons, and it seems fitting that it should be from the servants' area of the castle, for you wouldn't want to have to drag prisoners through the living quarters on their way to be incarcerated, would you? Sounds of pain and suffering do not sit well when one is entertaining.

'I believe we have our opportunity to explore what's down there, after nightfall and, as the castle is, at this moment, almost empty, I suggest we go to the cellars and have a good look around there, while the coast is clear.'

'Is there any lighting down there?' asked Lady A, stuffing her sandwiches down her throat as if she were in an eating competition.

'I believe there are some of those flaming torches, but I'd suggest we take electric torches. We might have to get out quickly, and, if we've lighted torches, they'll be a dead giveaway,' he commented, lapsing into the vernacular in his excitement. 'I believe I can supply all of us from the emergency kit in the Rolls.' He had also changed recently, but Lady A put it down to the fact that the truth about his parenthood was now common knowledge in Belchester Towers.

'Now you know why I have such a large handbag, Hugo,' Lady A told her friend, who was always moaning that she had room in its capacious interior for a hundredweight of coal, with space left over for the kitchen sink. 'I can put four torches in my bag without anyone noticing anything odd. Think how we'd look, just in case someone did see us, trotting off to the cellars, each carrying a torch. It would be frightfully suspicious.'

Hugo had to admit defeat on this occasion. A large handbag could be a very useful accessory when one had something to keep hidden. Finishing off his sandwiches, he rubbed his hands together with glee, and asked when they were setting off on this particular adventure.

'I would suggest as soon as Enid and I have returned the tray to the kitchen. We should still have quite a bit of time before anyone returns when the light starts to go. If

Lady Siobhan is discovered and brought back, everyone will be in a mood of such relief that no one will notice where we are, or what we're doing, in their mood of euphoria. Come along Enid. You can load the dishwasher while I rinse out the teapot.'

Within a quarter of an hour, they were inside the interior cellar door, Lady A surreptitiously handing out torches before they ventured any further into the dark. Beauchamp locked the door behind them, and they all four slunk inside and down the shallow flight of steps, keeping a keen eye out for anyone who might catch sight of them, but they proved to be totally alone.

The interior of the room smelt of damp and mould, and closer inspection revealed an earth floor. This part of the castle had, in all probability, not been altered since the place was built.

One by one the orbs of light descended, bringing into view a rough stone interior that was quite large, and contained, near the door, the remains of what had, at one time, been quite an extensive cellar. The few dozen bottles of wine that were still stored there were of superb quality and vintage, but they hid the secret of the room behind this more conventional screen of respectability.

Behind were rows and rows of bottles of the illegal spirit brewed in the forest, those in the front bearing labels, those to the back still awaiting this badge of apparent verity. In one corner, a table cowered in the darkness, its top covered in an assortment of labels, a small cabinet beside it containing what looked like a variety of greatly condensed flavourings.

This was the heart of the operation, with easy access, large storage space, and privacy; for who else would ever come in here, with this being a dry house, except Sir Cardew himself and his co-conspirators? It was the perfect set-up for the bottling and labelling of illegally manufactured liquor.

Entering the room that had access from the exterior of the castle, they found large plastic containers filled with a clear fluid, stacks of empty bottles, funnels, even a deep Belfast sink so that bottles could be sterilised before being filled. It was apparent that this operation was not a start-up side-line, but must have been in existence for some considerable time.

It seemed probable that Siobhan had not been aware of it, for they could not believe that, if she had suspected what was going on down here, she would keep quiet about it. She was a very honest woman who, quite obviously, lived in an otherworldly way, with her mind above such sordid things as had been going on in the castle itself, as well as out in the forest. She would have been mortified, had she been aware of such criminal goings-on.

'I think we should adjourn to our rooms for a rest now,' Beauchamp suggested. 'We don't want to chance our arms any further at this juncture.' There he went again, resorting to the vernacular. He just wasn't one to use slangy language, and now he'd done it twice in one day.

It was a sensible suggestion, though, and they obediently slunk out of the cellar rooms, leaving the manservant to lock up. Enid decided that she would have a lie down in her room as well, and the three of them left Beauchamp to his own devices, with an arrangement to dine at six-thirty from the cold collation left out, and meet again in Lady Amanda's room at midnight.

The search party trickled back in ones and twos, no sign having been found of Siobhan, or any clue to her whereabouts, and the cold collation was consumed in a gloomy silence. The only thing that could be said for dining a la buffet was that the food was rather more edible than some of the hot dishes had been. The Cullen skink and haggis had been the last really good things the party had eaten, with the exception of the Belchester Four, who had dined on smoked salmon sandwiches, with just a hint of horseradish mayonnaise, at luncheon.

After-dinner conversation also proved not to be brisk, and the only animated conversation to be seen, for it took place at a distance from which no one could hear it, was between Grizzly Rizzly and Wallace Menzies. They may have taken the decision not to stand somewhere where they could be eavesdropped upon, but they looked to Lady Amanda just like villains in a cheap Victorian melodrama plotting the overthrow of the hero, and Hugo agreed with her when she broached the subject.

Knowing what time they had planned for their meeting, Hugo and Lady Amanda took themselves off to bed very early, in the hope that they could complement their afternoon naps with a little pre-exploratory sleep. They had to take account of their age, and they didn't know how long they would be out of their beds in the wee small hours.

At five minutes to midnight, Beauchamp knocked discreetly on Lady Amanda's door and was bidden to enter, in a low voice that indicated that her ladyship was up and about, and wouldn't need wakening. The manservant was greatly relieved, because not only was waking his half-sister a thankless task – in that she slept like the dead – but if woken before she was ready, meant that she acted like a bear with a sore head, until midday.

A discreet knock on the door of Hugo's adjoining room produced no response, and Beauchamp, after two more attempts, was forced to open the door and hiss at the lump under the covers to wake up, for it was time to go. This also produced no response and, eventually, he had to shake Hugo's unconscious form, quite vigorously, to get any response.

'Whassup?' asked Hugo blearily.

'It's time to wake up. We have to leave, now, Mr

Hugo,' Beauchamp replied, patiently.

'Wake up? I wasn't asleep! Couldn't get off at all. Damned cheek, thinking a fellow's asleep, when he can't get a wink.'

'You were snoring, Mr Hugo, with respect.'

'I was?'

'Very loudly, as it happens.'

''Straordinary! Was I really? Well, well, well! Amazing what one can do and not know a thing about it. Sorry about that, old chap. Give me five minutes or so, and I'll come through to Her Nibs' room.'

Lady Amanda was wearing a pair of black stretch trousers and a black jumper for, as she always said, if one goes away, it's as well to go prepared for a funeral, when one's friends are the age of hers. Beauchamp was similarly attired in black, knowing that anything pale would pick up any light that there was, and pinpoint them immediately, if someone were looking out for them.

When Hugo finally appeared, he had on the same light beige slacks, white shirt, and oatmeal jacket that he had worn during the day. 'HUGO!' hissed Lady Amanda, with real exasperation in the word. 'Just what do you think you're wearing?'

'What I had on earlier. I didn't want to soil anything fresh, and this is likely to be a messy job if we're going down to the dungeons,' he replied, with perfect logic – perfect logic for the daytime, maybe, but not for their secret explorations at this time of night.

'Think about it, man! If you go out dressed like that, you'll positively shine from any light source. We don't want to be discovered poking around where some believe we have no business to be. Go back to your room and put on the darkest clothes you've got!' she ordered him, in an imperious hiss.

'Sorry! Didn't really think it through, did I?' he intoned in a voice full of chagrin. He hated to be found wanting, and his garb was rather ridiculous, when one thought about it.

He reappeared after a considerable amount of drawer-opening and shutting, and rather a lot of mild cussing, wearing a pair of slate grey trousers and an old navy pullover. His reaction to their glances at the vintage of his jumper was to say, in mitigation, 'Sometimes I wear it in bed over my pyjamas, if it's particularly cold. In fact, I've got my pyjamas on under this lot. It's probably darned chilly down in those dungeons.'

Lady Amanda picked up her black handbag containing the torches and, just as they were about to go, Enid arrived, huffing and puffing. 'Sorry I'm late,' she said. 'I set my alarm and put it under the pillow so I wouldn't wake anyone else, but the dratted thing was a quarter of an hour slow. The battery must be running out. Sorry, sorry, sorry!'

'That's all right. We'd have given you a knock on the way past. I see you've sensibly dressed in dark colours,' said Lady A.

'Of course! Light-coloured clothing would be asking for trouble, wouldn't it?' she asked, and Hugo had the grace to blush, even though neither of the other two said a word about his first attempt at dressing for underhand deeds.

Before they could get out of the room, however, there was a rumbling sound from outside, and a screech of elderly brakes outside the window, and they all stopped short. That sounded very like the arrival of an elderly lorry, and three of them approached the window with caution, Lady Amanda staying behind to switch off the light before the curtains were drawn back.

There, illuminated in the starlight, was a truck big enough to hold everything they had discovered in the cellar rooms, and more. Someone they could not identify got out and unlocked the exterior cellar door; his passenger, just as unidentifiable, followed and, between them, they started loading the moonshine into the back of the vehicle.

'Oh my God!' Lady A exclaimed quietly. 'It looks like they're clearing out. This must be a reaction to Sir Cardew's death. We've got to get away from here before they go off to fetch Lady Siobhan. If everything's gone wrong for them, she may be killed like Cardew – if she's not already dead.'

'Leave this bit to me,' said Beauchamp, with determination in his voice. 'You three wait here. I'll only be gone a short time – ten minutes at the very most.'

'Where are you going?' asked Lady Amanda.

'What are you going to do?' queried Hugo.

'You're not going to do anything dangerous, are you?' pleaded Enid.

'I'm just going to put their truck out of action,' he replied to them all.

'How?' This was Lady Amanda again.

'I'll tell you when I've done it, to save valuable time now. The longer they're stuck here, the longer we have to try to rescue the damsel in distress, and summon outside help to round the blackguards up.'

'Damsel, my big fat hairy bottom!' floated out of the door after him, as Lady A made her feelings clear about there being any resemblance whatsoever between Siobhan and a maiden.

He was gone only eight minutes, and explained that he had gone down to the kitchen for a bag of sugar, which he had then poured into the petrol tank of the old vehicle. He had also collected a potato from the vegetable store, and shoved that up the exhaust pipe for good measure, having been lucky enough to arrive during a short period of the villains' absence in the cellars. 'I did hear them mention Lady Siobhan, though,' he told them, 'so I think our window of opportunity is short.'

This quickly conjured up tale of horror galvanised even Hugo, and they decided that there should be no delay in them commencing their search of the dungeon regions.

Chapter Nine

They stepped quietly out of the room, finding only one torchere burning at the stairs end of the corridor, but Beauchamp steered them the other way, explaining, 'Best to use the back stairs. Someone might not be able to sleep, and might have got up for a late nightcap.' As he spoke, Hugo grabbed a small hunting horn from the wall and stuffed it into the capacious pocket of his disgraceful woolly, with no thought of what he would do with it, but just a vague idea that it might prove useful.

'That's nowhere near as likely with one of the staff,' the manservant continued, 'they're usually whacked by ten o'clock, not just because they have to work so hard in this stone maze, but because they have to get up so early, with there being so few of them, to light fires, make early morning tea, and all the other chores to which owners of properties like these never give a thought.'

'Nice grammar,' hissed Enid, following closely on his heels.

'Good God, it's spooky on these old back stairs.' Hugo, no hero in the dark, was more nervous of ghosts than he had ever been in his life, because of his two experiences during the night on this trip.

'Grow a backbone,' whispered Lady A, unsympathetically.

'Please could we have a little quiet, until we get to the trapdoor? We need to listen carefully, in case there's anyone else about.' This was Beauchamp feeling rather like an infants' school teacher on a school outing, in charge of a small group of unruly charges.

Totally ignoring this order, Hugo asked, with a quiver in his voice, 'What's that tapping noise,' fearful that they might be in the company of a spirit who had been walled up on the staircase, hundreds of years ago, and was still waiting for his remains to be found.

'It's your walking stick!' – Lady Amanda, in exasperation.

'Damn! Silly me!' – Hugo, once more embarrassed.

'Is it much further?' – Enid, who wasn't very fond of confined spaces, and this staircase was very confined indeed. They were almost treading on each other's heels.

'Ssssh!' – Beauchamp, in incomprehension at their inability to obey a simple order.

Somehow, they made it to the foot of the winding stone staircase without mishap, and made their way, as silently as four people who are in a state of fearful anticipation can, and Beauchamp led them to the scullery, where the mat had now been moved, to cover the trapdoor he had found earlier.

He was just about to lift it and reveal the hidden staircase, when a noise produced little yips of fear from three of the party, and they all froze as if they were playing the old-fashioned children's game of musical statues. The fear of discovery coursed through all their veins, as they wondered who it could be that had rumbled their plan.

Could it be Grizzly Rizzly? Menzies? Were they here already? Was it possible they had already cleared out their contraband? Surely there hadn't been sufficient time for them to move all that gear? If it were one of them, they were in real trouble. Maybe he, or they, if it were both of them, really did have Siobhan hidden down below, and were coming to fetch her?

They hadn't thought the chances were very high that they might actually be right about where the miscreants had stashed their hostess. It was surely more likely that they would have used one of the out-of-the-way bothies for such a purpose. This was really supposed to be a bit of an adventure, not a life-threatening experience. What would be done to them? Would they, too, be kidnapped; or hurt; or even killed?

Lady Amanda felt as if her head would burst, and Hugo was certain that his heartbeat was as loud as that of a big bass drum. And, as for Enid, she was shaking so much she could hardly stand, and feared that she might faint with fear and trepidation. Only Beauchamp remained calm, out of sheer habit.

Eight eyes swivelled round in the direction from which the noise had come, their gaze acknowledged by, 'Meow!'

'It's the bloody cat!' exclaimed Lady A, breaking her own rule of never swearing. The object of their relief wandered haughtily over to the range, and flopped down in front of it to worship the source of the heat, then swept a languid tongue over the fur of one of its front paws, having no idea what terror his night-time entrance had caused. He was just glad he had found a way in, and no one had, so far, attempted to eject him.

Sighs of relief echoed round the scullery, as Lady Amanda handed out the torches, and Beauchamp led the way down the steep stone steps, hissing, 'Mind your footing. The steps are steeper than you might think.'

At the bottom of the steps, they thought they were to be thwarted by the presence of a locked door, but Beauchamp was one step ahead of the others, and had spent his free time that evening after they had retired for a pre-adventure nap, searching for any large key that he could lay his hands on, just in case the one he had located earlier did not fit. He had quite a few, in this eventuality, but the original one he had found in the cellars did the job successfully, and granted them entrance.

Torches were turned on, while the manservant opened the door, surprised to find that, not only had the key turned easily, but that the door swung open without a creak. The hinges must have been recently oiled, to produce no resistance whatsoever. The chances of finding Siobhan suddenly went up several rungs of the ladder of luck.

The first area that they passed through smelt similarly of damp, earth and decay for, after all, who would think of making dungeons comfortable and sweet-smelling? Piles of mouldering sacks lay around the place, as did broken chairs and tables, with rats scurrying hither and thither, surprised by this unexpected visit to the one place they called their own, by two-legged giants.

Enid made a series of 'ee, ee, ee', noises, in fear and disgust, sounding rather like a rat herself, and hopped around, trying to achieve the impossible act of keeping both her feet off the ground at the same time. To add to this distraction, Hugo was also doing his best to jump around, issuing distressing little noises of disgust. 'I say, Manda, this place is absolutely crawling with arachnids, and you know I've got a phobia about the eight-legged little horrors.'

'Can it, Enid! Be a man, Hugo! They can't hurt you,' ordered the less squeamish Lady A, and shone her torch around the dismal chamber.

'But rats can bite and scratch, and they carry disease,' whined Enid, still doing her best to levitate.

'Just look straight in front of you, and ignore them.' Lady Amanda was not putting up with this childish behaviour, when they were on an important mission. Fortunately, at that point in the proceedings, her torch hit paydirt, so to speak, bringing to light another stout wooden door in the opposite wall. 'Over there, Beauchamp,' she indicated, leaving the yellowish orb of her torch-light to dwell on the further barrier.

He responded by jingling the collection of keys he had brought with him, and shining his own torch to light his way over the uneven floor. 'We'll soon have that open,' he informed her, with confidence, and proceeded to try the keys again, one by one. While he was thus engaged, they heard a feeble sound from within this second chamber, which sounded very like someone calling for help; someone female.

'By George, I think we've got her!' exclaimed Lady A, rushing over to join him.

Beauchamp, finding the right key, opened the door gingerly, worried that there might be someone in there with Siobhan, if it was Siobhan, but the moving door caused no calls of alarm or threat, and they followed him into the darkness of a large chamber, in a corner of which was their hostess, in chains and rather grubby, due to her unexpected holiday in this unfrequented part of her domain.

'Thank God you've come at last!' she exclaimed. 'Mind the commode! You don't need light to find it; your noses can do that job adequately enough.'

'There are never any commodes in films, when someone's locked away and kept prisoner,' commented Hugo, absent-mindedly, to keep his mind off the spiders. 'I've always wondered how they coped, when someone was locked up for a long time.'

'Hugo, don't be coarse,' replied Lady Amanda, then added, 'But you do actually have a point. They're not like real life, those films. They just ignore the nitty-gritty, which is ridiculous, when you think about it. I mean, everyone's got to "go", haven't they?'

Picking their way over the uneven earth of the floor, and avoiding the large lumps of masonry that had been dumped down here for some long-forgotten reason, Beauchamp produced a small hip flask and held it to the prisoner's lips.

'We'll soon have you out of here,' promised Lady A. 'All we have to do is alert Inspector Glenister, and he'll be here in a jiffy, with something to cut through those chains. Beauchamp can sort that out, and the rest of us will stay with you. Cut along there, Beauchamp, old chap, and fetch the cavalry, please.'

Beauchamp cut along, and the other three tried to comfort poor Siobhan, who had been cold, hungry, thirsty, and, above all, terrified that she would not live to tell the tale of her abduction. They managed to get her to her feet, leaving their torches balanced on pieces of stone to light them adequately, then Enid and Lady A massaged her hands and arms, and Hugo put his arm round her waist to help her regain her balance.

As they were thus engaged, there was a noise at the door of the room, and Ralf Colcolough strolled in, not showing any surprise at the presence of the kidnapped woman and her rescuers. 'Thank God you're here, Mr Colcolough,' said Lady Amanda. Perhaps you can help Siobhan regain her balance, because Hugo here's not very strong and …'

Looking at the expression on his face, as he crossed the chamber and entered the lit circle, she realised that he was not a member of the cavalry, but a previously unsuspected member of the gang, and her blood ran cold. The 'third man' was not a woodsman, after all. He was another of the guests, and he would lock them all in here and leave them. She had to let the others know not to tell him that Beauchamp had gone for help, or he'd hunt him down after he'd dealt with them.

'I wish my manservant had come with us tonight,' she declared, in ringing tones, with particular emphasis on the wording of her coded message. 'He'd have known what to do. Such a pity that he stayed in bed,' she said with even greater emphasis, partly to warn the others, and to make Colcolough think that she hadn't twigged yet that he was not on their side.

Hugo began to say something, but received a vicious kick on the ankle, just out of the circle of light, and fell silent in rather a huff. He didn't know why he'd been silenced and was willing to trust Lady A's judgement, but did she have to kick quite so hard? Why was she telling this nice man, who had come to their rescue, that Beauchamp was in bed, ill? She must be going mad.

'Yes, that's a really dreadful cold he's come down with,' piped up Enid, who had been quicker on the uptake than Hugo. 'He was as weak as a kitten when dear Lady Amanda let him off duty early.' Now Enid was at it as well, and Hugo set his mind to unravelling why both women were determined to deny the fact that Beauchamp had been with them, until just a few minutes ago.

Suddenly, Hugo realised what was going on, although he didn't know why the two ladies wanted to conceal the fact that Beauchamp would soon be on his way back, so he put in his two-penn'orth. 'Poor chap could hardly speak, and his nose was as bright as a beacon, sweat running off him.' He might not fully comprehend what was in their minds, but the least he could do was support them in their insistence.

'I'm so glad you've come to our rescue. Perhaps you'd be good enough to alert the inspector that we've found Siobhan, and we can get on with cutting her out of these barbaric irons,' twittered Lady A, having no intention of alerting him to the fact that he'd been outed as 'batting for the other side', in more ways than one.

'Oh, I'm not here to rescue you,' he drawled, curling his upper lip into a left-sided sneer. 'I'm here to eliminate you. Did you really have no idea? It was to be only one more death, but now you three have turned up, I don't see how that's possible. I think, on the whole, the best plan would be to lock you all down here. This place was built a very long time ago, and, even then, they didn't want the sounds of suffering from the dungeons to permeate to the living quarters of the castle.'

The trio of new captives blanched, although this was not obvious in the little light that was available to them

They had never suspected this particular guest as being in on the racket, and they all knew they would have to think on their feet, to try to extricate themselves from this perilous situation. Unusually, it was Hugo who girded his loins first.

'You can't do that, you utter cad!' he spat, suddenly becoming aware of the whole game that the two women had been playing, and identifying the man as an unexpected enemy.

'Oh, I think you'll find that I can. I don't know how you got through the door at the bottom of the steps from the scullery, or through into here, but this door opens outwards. I wonder if you realise what that means. All I have to do is to get a couple of the others, and barricade it with the boulders strewn around the place, and you'll never get out.'

As he spoke, Lady Amanda's fear slipped away, to be replaced with a blind, red rage. How dare he treat his hostess like that! How dare he tell them, so languidly and callously, that they were all going to die in this hole, and that there was nothing they could do about it! Well, Beauchamp was on his way back, and that'd stir things up a bit. Little did she know quite how much they would be shaken, in the next half-hour.

'There'll be no commode services for you; or food and water, as Lady Siobhan has had,' he continued, with brazen insolence. 'It'll be black as night, and if you don't die of hypothermia, given your ages, you'll starve, but eventually die of dehydration.'

Now, he really looked as if he was enjoying himself, the perverted, treacherous oaf, and anger began to stir in Enid, too. She might be an insignificant person in the great scheme of things, but she had plans for the rest of her life, and she had no intentions of being deprived of that time, because of some small-time crook, no matter how toffee-nosed he appeared to be.

'It's a particularly unpleasant and long-drawn-out way to die, but if you play the game, you've got to be prepared to take the consequences, and this was a particularly dangerous game to get involved with. You're going to die down here, in awful pain, and your last breath will be filled with the stink of your own waste, not that there'll be much of that, after a day or two, when you're all husked out,' he concluded, casually pulling a gun from his jacket pocket, and leering at them triumphantly.

'And I expect this little fellow here,' he said, brandishing his weapon, 'will dissuade you from trying to overpower me. The first one who moves in my direction will be signing dear Siobhan's death warrant.'

'What a bounder you are, sir,' Hugo growled, now also full of fury at the way they had been trapped. Ralf Colcolough didn't know it, but he was now holding at bay three dangerously angry old-age pensioners.

'May your black soul rot in hell!' Lady Amanda cursed him.

'May you have long, dangling external haemorrhoids' spat Enid, drawing the puzzled eyes of her two companions. 'Well, it's the worst thing I could think of. If you've ever suffered from them, as I have, you'll know just what an evil curse that was,' she justified herself.

'Not a moment without pain, day or night, and a hospital waiting list to get through, before you can get anything done about them.' She paused after this explanation, remembering the suffering she had gone through, and how surgery had given her the greatest relief from pain she had ever known.

As Colcolough drew breath to reply, there was a shout from the doorway and, just discernible in the dim borrowed light from the circle of torches, stood two figures, both appearing to hold double-barrelled shotguns. Who had arrived now? Friend or foe? It was impossible to tell until they approached the light.

'Armed police!' yelled the voice of Inspector Glenister, who was accompanied by PC MacDuff. 'Drop that gun, or we'll fire!' Thank God the cavalry had arrived, but where on earth was Beauchamp? thought Lady Amanda, now thoroughly alarmed for her manservant's safety.

Colcolough sulkily complied with the order, as two shotguns outranked one pistol. 'Now kick it away from you!' Glenister ordered, as he and the constable moved further into the chamber. Once again the miscreant complied. He'd evidently been thinking, however, for he now didn't look either crestfallen or defeated.

'I'm going to send PC MacDuff over to you to handcuff you, and if you resist, it will be my pleasure to shoot you, you murdering swine.' Glenister didn't mince his words. How dare this fop threaten three elderly people in this way? It was barbaric!

But before MacDuff could move, yet another voice sounded behind him. It was that of Menzies and, as they turned, they became aware of both him and Wriothesley standing behind them aiming pistols at them.

'I think not, Inspector. This is way off your beat. You're in our manor now, and we run things, not you.' Colcolough retrieved his gun, and it was now three firearms against two, in his favour. The stakes were getting higher, and there didn't seem to be anyone to trump the enemies' ace.

'My God!' exclaimed Lady A. 'This is the first time I've ever seen a real Mexican stand-o ff. I thought they only happened in films. I shall be most interested to see what happens next.' Her words were brave, and her temper still sky-high, but that still didn't stop her stomach churning with apprehension.

There was no way out of this predicament that she could see, without someone being either seriously hurt, or even killed. Yet, she still had a little something up her sleeve that might prove useful, given the circumstances to utilise it. If only Beauchamp were unharmed and would return soon, she thought, sending up a little prayer of forlorn hope, to whoever might be listening.

Chapter Ten

Yet another voice, from the now deserted doorway, suddenly rang out round the chamber, refined and confident. 'Anyone for cocktails? I've mixed a good selection,' and there stood Beauchamp with a large silver tray in his hands, loaded with full glasses of every hue imaginable.

This unexpected event riveted all eyes on the new arrival, astonishment evident on each of the three criminals' faces at such an extraordinary thing happening: to bring cocktails to what was going to be either a series of executions, or an incarceration until death. Was the man completely out of his mind? Had he risen from his sick-bed and decided that cocktails were just the thing, if only he could locate his mistress?

Beauchamp looked Lady Amanda straight in the eyes, and widened his just enough to let her know that it was time for action. They might not have made any verbal plans, but the shared genes must have linked them mentally, somehow, for she behaved exactly how he'd needed her to.

He had been sidling across the room to the more recent entrants with his tray, as he offered his drinks. 'Roman Candle? Brandy Alexander? Grasshopper? Manhattan? Blue Lagoon? Can I not tempt any of you with this fine selection of cocktails? They're on the tray just waiting to be drunk,' he called out, like a refined fairground barker.

Lady Amanda suddenly kicked Hugo again, and as he began to yell, turning all eyes in his direction, Beauchamp yelled too ('Geronimo!' in fact) and threw the contents of his tray into the faces of Menzies and Wriothesley, and they flicked back in his direction, as his cry had been a fraction of a second after Hugo's cry of pain and incomprehension, at being assaulted yet again, with no apparent cause, and no warning whatsoever.

Hugo's loud acknowledgement of pain was followed immediately by a piercing scream from Lady Amanda, and all the confusion caused Enid to start shrieking too. As the echoes of the sounds of the assault on the silent cavern, of four different voices died away, a completely different configuration held sway.

Hugo suddenly remembered the hunting horn, and gave a blast on it that would be enough to raise the dead, then descended into a fit of coughing at the amount of breath he had had to use to produce the sound.

In the confusion, Enid kneed Colcolough in the unmentionables. No way was she going to give up what she had planned for her future, and no one would take that away from her. Beauchamp, his belly aflame with determination, bashed Menzies over the head with his heavy tray, denting it in his enthusiasm, then both he and Lady Amanda drew guns. Lady A held a small mother-of-pearl-handled pistol, and Beauchamp had retrieved a slightly larger version from a special pocket in his tailcoat.

Both had independently decided to bring along a weapon and, although Beauchamp knew all about Lady Amanda's dangerous little trinket, she had no idea that he carried such a weapon in his everyday uniform of tailcoat and pin-striped trousers. Neither knew why they had brought their guns with them, but instinct had suggested that something might occur when they would be advantageous. Some hunches should be taken seriously, and this had been one of those, born of shared blood.

Both Glenister and MacDuff had turned their shotguns towards the two men who were now doubled over, groaning with pain, and Lady A had one well covered. She was feeling very ticked off that none of them had identified Colcolough as being part of the gang, and she took this personally. How dare he fool her for this long!

'In our pockets,' said Glenister with urgency, 'we have a pair of handcuffs each. Take them, Beauchamp, and use them to link the three together. That'll hold them till we get back upstairs where we can tie them up individually, while we get an explanation of what all this has been about.'

The inspector did his best to sound butch and masculine, but he had had to get Cook to open the gun room for him to get the shotguns, and he was uneasy with any firearms, especially ones he held himself, but only the slightest of tremors gave away his state of mind, given the fact that the shotguns were not loaded, and had only ever been intended to act as a bluff.

'But we know ...' Lady Amanda started to utter, but was immediately silenced by Glenister.

'I know you probably know every little detail, but I need it from the horses' mouths, so just keep shtum for now. Remember, I know your reputation from talking to my nephew, and I'll give you the opportunity to let me know just how clever you've been, later, when I've got the goods from this little lot.'

'Before we all leave this delightful area of the castle,' she cut in, 'I suggest that you have a word with Macdonald. I'm sure there's someone else involved, and someone from the outside staff would fit the bill admirably. Don't ask questions, just do it!' I'll explain when you've got him; or rather they'll do that for you.

'They could never have run this little scam without someone who really knew the castle and the woods like the back of his hand, and Cardew didn't know the woods sufficiently. They also needed someone who would not be out of place anywhere on the estate, or in the less used parts of the castle.

'Who would suspect a head game-keeper? He'd need to be inside to consult his employer, check the guns and ammunition, and for meals and refreshments. He's rather like a postman – not even noticed as a person in his own right; just someone that one would expect to see about, just getting on with his job.

'Mind the broken glasses as you go out, and I suggest you let these three go first, Inspector. If Macdonald has got wind of this, he'll be waiting at the top of the stairs. Just tell them to be as silent as the grave or you'll plug one of them. And if you don't, I will. They can't get far, all handcuffed together like that.'

With a smile of superiority on her face, she muttered, 'Well done, Beauchamp! That really was thinking outside the tantalus, let alone the box.'

Macdonald hadn't proved difficult to locate. He knew that the racket was clearing out of the castle and, therefore, his domain, and he was making the most of his last opportunity to be a taster for the product they had manufactured.

He'd made himself scarce during the loading of the lorry, and had been drinking in solitude in the servant's hall, when Lady A et al had gone down the dungeon steps. It was he who had alerted Colcolough, and then been sent off to find the other two. While he waited for them to emerge, he had sipped his way rapidly into an alcoholic stupor at the great kitchen table, and it was there they found him now, the bottle knocked over by his arm, his head on the wood, snoring the snore of the absolutely blotto.

'Cook's OK,' Beauchamp announced, apropos of nothing, but was understood perfectly by Glenister, who also believed Cook to be on the side of the angels, since it was she who had given him access to the arms he and MacDuff had used to bluff their way through the potential disaster that never materialised, down in the dungeons.

'When we've got this little lot's hash settled,' he pronounced, 'I'll send MacDuff to fetch her, and she can watch over him until reinforcements arrive. I've already put out a call, but we're not being treated to any more fancy and expensive choppers. The minor roads are all clear now, so they'll be arriving by road.

We spent quite a bit of time down in the dungeons playing 'who's going to shoot first', so I don't think she'll have long to stand guard before they get here, then she can get back to bed.'

'I doubt she'll do that, Inspector. Knowing Cook, she'll want the ins and outs of a duck's arse, before she'll rest.'

'ENID!' bellowed Lady A, and the head gamekeeper twitched in his sleep. 'Where did you learn language like that?'

'From my mother,' Mrs Tweedie replied, with a smile of sweet innocence on her face.

'Well, I'll be jiggered!' exclaimed Lady A, in flabbergasted tones, and followed the others to the library, where there was sufficient seating for them all, including an extra-long and extremely uncomfortable sofa, to accommodate the three who were joined together with a bond that was, without a key, unbreakable, and probably a darned sight stronger than the loose business arrangement they had been enjoying, from what was now, and always had been, Lady Siobhan's estate.

As it turned out, the three aristocratic co-conspirators couldn't wait to rat on each other, and the tale of the manufacture and distribution of the moonshine was soon unravelling with a plethora of cross-accusations about who had done what.

It was as Lady Amanda and the gang had suspected. The illegal liquor was made in the still in the forest, then transported to the castle cellar. There, it was bottled and labelled, and flavour was added, so that the product had some variety.

After that, it was collected by lorry, courtesy of Menzies' haulage business, and taken to the coast, where it was ferried over to an agreed spot in the wilds of the Irish coast, boats courtesy of Wriothesley's so-called fishing business. The only mystery was how the slimy Colcolough fitted into the deal, and he gave this information to them of his own free will.

He was the money man. Both the haulage business and the fishing business of two of the partners had been in a parlous state, and he had been persuaded to invest in what they were doing, in order to get them each out of a financial hole. Cardew was similarly financially embarrassed, having enjoyed a fondness for horseracing and poker, about which Siobhan had known nothing, as he indulged in both of these gambling activities via the internet. He had been more than happy to offer the castle and its estate for the manufacture of the product.

The money was split four ways, with a small remuneration to Macdonald, for his part in their nefarious activities, which had been going on for a few years now.

'But why the murders?' asked Glenister, genuinely interested in how the piper had got involved, and what had caused the fall-out that resulted in Sir Cardew's bizarre murder.

'Jock Macleod overheard us planning to move the latest batch. My God, what an innocent the man was.' This was Grizzly Rizzly speaking, and he appeared eager to share the simple honesty of the ex-piper with them as an act of unbelievable folly. 'He ought to have asked for a "wee cut", as he'd no doubt have referred to it, and he'd probably have got away with that. The poor lad, though, threatened to turn us over to the police. He had no idea what danger he was putting himself in.'

They were all quick to point the finger at Macdonald

for the murder of the piper, but they fought like dogs over who had dropped the broadsword so accurately on Cardew, thus turning him into a giant, human, late-Saturday-night-snack of meat on a skewer. It was still stomach-churning even to think about what he had looked like, and it appeared as if the three were on the verge of blaming that on Macdonald as well, when the small sinewy man himself joined them, hanging by the scruff of his neck from the ham-like hand of Cook.

He looked to be in a bad way, still blurry with sleep, and still suffering more than a little from the effects of his ingestion of the illegal alcohol. She dumped him unceremoniously on the sofa, saying, 'Yer wee man woke up, so I thought he ought to join the party, as he was one of the party-planners in the first place,' before stumping out of the room to take a look at Siobhan, who had been sent straight to bed, with the doctor summoned to check her over.

Cook had no intention whatsoever of waking Evelyn Waule, and retiring to her bed, where she'd miss any of the excitement still to come, if she didn't have to. That way, she'd have a real tale to tell at breakfast, and she'd be the centre of attention for some time to come, as well as making Evelyn as jealous as hell, that it had been her who had looked after the lady of the house, and not her, her own lady's maid.

Picking up the threads of where he had been in his questioning, Glenister next asked, 'Why did you kill Cardew? Was there a falling out between you?'

'You bet there was,' replied Colcolough. 'I put up the money to get this thing started, and provided the contacts across the water, but when I sneaked a look at the books, when Cardew was otherwise engaged, I could see he was skimming off money for his own personal use.

'A quick break-in of his computer, with a well-guessed password – he never was cunning enough for this sort of life – clearly showed that he had a bank account in the Cayman Islands, and there was a ticket in his desk, one way. He was going to have it on his toes with the majority of the money, leaving us to take the rap should word ever get out. What a bastard! He got no more than he deserved!'

'And so shall you, Mr Colcolough. So shall you, along with your partners in crime.' This statement hadn't quite the drama that Glenister expected, as it was accompanied by loud snores and snorts from Macdonald, who had fallen asleep the moment he settled on the sofa Cook had dropped him on. 'And he's in for a shock when he wakes up,' the inspector concluded, glaring at the old man who had just rained on his parade.

'But who was the woman in all this?' asked Hugo, eager to solve his own personal mystery.

'What woman?' asked Menzies, as all three of the handcuffed men looked puzzled.

'When you were about your night-time activities, moving the stuff about. Manda and I sleep on that side of the castle, and have rooms that overlook the exterior to the door to where you stored your hooch.

'Twice, I woke up to find a woman in a black veil leaning over me, while I'd been sleeping, so I assumed she was just checking that neither of us was awake. She wouldn't have woken Manda, because she sleeps like the dead, but she woke me and scared the living daylights out of me.'

'There was no woman!' exclaimed Colcolough indignantly.

'We'd never trust a woman with that sort of secret!' declared Menzies with fervour.

'Nothing to do with us,' confirmed Wriothesley. 'You must have been dreaming. Nobody checked on any of the guests to see if they were sleeping.'

Hugo went as white as a sheet, and clammed up like an

oyster – or a clam, come to think of it. He'd have to pretend he hadn't heard those emphatic denials, if he were to spend any more time in this ancient building, and there was no way he was going to sleep in that room again. No way!

At that juncture, the police summoned to help take the three reported, but now four, men into custody arrived with a van. The danger had passed, but they had with them a police marksman, in case a state of siege had been in existence when they arrived. Thanks to Beauchamp and Lady Amanda, this had been prevented, but the armed policeman might have proved very useful if half-brother and sister hadn't thought to come armed on this visit, with nothing but a hunch to cause them so to do.

With the wrong-doers in custody and out of the castle, the stragglers decided that it was necessary for them to get at least a few hours' sleep, so that they would be fresh to speak to Siobhan in the morning, to get her side of the story.

Cook reappeared after the van had left, and informed them that she had stripped the rooms of the three no-longer-present guests, for use by the police, should they wish to take advantage of the accommodation. They would be much more comfortable there than in the cots that had been put out for them in an empty staff bedroom, and both the inspector and the constable agreed with alacrity, being dead on their feet, without actually being deceased, which had been a distinct possibility earlier on in the night.

Hugo, who was still as silent as the grave, asked if he might use one of the rooms, as he had taken a sudden dislike to his quarters, and could do with a change, and was given the thumbs-up. And that was everything that could be done, dealt with for the night.

As they left, to go upstairs, Lady Amanda turned to her old friend and said, 'Hugo, that blast on that horn was completely off-the-wall. Where did you get it?'

'Yes!' replied Hugo, enigmatically, and disappeared into the room he was about to vacate.

There, he collected his necessary possessions for spending the night in a different room, and retired to bed tired, but unworried about surprise night-time visitors. He had only been asleep for an hour, however, when the strident skirl of the pipes woke him, and he was so incensed, that he waited for the piper to round the castle and, when he was just below his window, hurled his alarm clock at him with great accuracy, and a roar to 'Bloody well shut up!'

There was a cry of pain, followed by the dismal sound of a set of pipes deflating, and Hugo was, at last, able to get some well-earned rest.

Chapter Eleven

None of those involved in the previous night's caper woke before noon, and didn't arrive downstairs until nearly one o'clock. The doctor had called, hours earlier, to examine Siobhan, to check that she had suffered no long-lasting harm from her incarceration, and she had ventured downstairs just before noon.

By the time the other guests involved in the previous night's activities appeared, she had ordered lunch for one-thirty, and instructed Cook that dinner was now never to be served before eight. She was already taking over the reins of the running of the castle, and was raring to go, as far as the rest of the estate was concerned.

She had already summoned the outside staff and ordered them to remove all trace of the still, once the police had all the evidence they needed, and was already planning residential shooting parties in season, and a host of other activities that would support the running needs of the castle without resorting to crime. She was a woman reborn.

Once it had dawned on her that she and her husband lived totally separate lives, and that the love between them had been lost some time ago, she also woke up to the fact that the castle was, in fact, hers, and had never been his, to run. Not only did she intend to really live now, but she might even look for a like-minded partner who would share this brave new world with her, although she would never again contemplate marriage.

Without her heavy make-up and elaborate out-of-date hair-do, she looked ten years younger, and after the shock

169

of all that had happened, felt it as well, flooded with relief and gratitude to still be alive, and with the opportunity to rearrange her life to her own satisfaction.

'I've organised a celebratory dinner for tonight:' she informed her remaining guests at luncheon, 'one that will help to erase the terrible events that have taken place here during your stay, and perhaps encourage you to believe that Castle Rumdrummond isn't such a bad place after all. It will represent a wake for Cardew and Macleod, and celebrate the fact that I've got my common sense back, after years of living in a fugue state. I've also arranged for the piper to play for us, for some dancing.

'Funny, but he had a lump on his forehead when I spoke to him earlier, but he didn't seem to want to talk about how he got it.'

Hugo sat and blushed quietly to himself. He didn't feel in the least guilty; just justified. Just before luncheon was served, he toddled round to the side of the castle from which his room looked out, and retrieved his alarm clock, unharmed, from the bare twigs of a shrub, into which it had ricocheted from the piper's head. He slipped it to Beauchamp, whom he ran across on re-entry, to be returned to his new quarters, leaving no one any the wiser about how the piper had been injured.

Lunch proved to be a much jollier affair than usual, with a couple of bottles of the excellent wines that the amateur sleuths had discovered in the cellar sitting on the table for their enjoyment. Once again, Siobhan was in her element.

'I never really approved of this being a dry house,' she informed them. 'I have always been of the opinion that a man who doesn't drink has something to hide; that he would be afraid of what he might reveal under the influence of alcohol, and I seem to have been proved right.

'From now on, this is a normal household, which will have wines upon its table and sherry before dinner, for all

170

who wish to indulge. And as for that terrible bilge that Cardew insisted was served after dinner, I've had Cook pour it down the sink. From now on there will be port and brandy for all who want them.'

As they left the table, Lady A whispered to Hugo, 'I think we'll still indulge in our private cocktail session this evening, don't you? After all, we'll be going home tomorrow. Beauchamp and Enid will leave as soon as cocktails are partaken of, and we have flights booked for tomorrow afternoon. I took the liberty of using the telephone just before you came down, having apprised Beauchamp of my decision.'

'Oh, goody-goody-gumdrops!' exclaimed Hugo, with an unexpected return to nursery language. 'I do so miss our normal everyday life, and I shall be very grateful to get back to just pootling through life with no alarums and scares.' Hugo's memory could be very fickle at times. 'And now I think I'll go for another little snooze. Long night, what ho?'

At six-thirty sharp, Beauchamp and Enid entered Lady Amanda's room to find Hugo there, waiting for them, Lady Amanda sprawling in a chair before the blazing grate, half-asleep. The arrival of the drinks tray, however, soon had her back to full consciousness.

'I have taken the liberty of providing two turbo-charged Snowballs for the ladies, one a double for your ladyship, and a much smaller one for Enid. I have also brought a double Scotch Mist for Mr Hugo, and a rather more innocuous cocktail for myself – an Apple of my Eye – as I shall be driving after this last of our evening meetings.'

'Golly, you can sound pompous at times, Beechie, old stick,' Lady Amanda ragged him, then realised what she'd called him. 'Oh, I'm terribly sorry about that, Beauchamp. I didn't mean to offend you. I don't know what came over me!'

'No offence taken. And I did address you rather informally, twice, in the aftermath of my misadventure in the snow, so perhaps we ought to call it quits.' Although neither of them would admit it, they both felt a half-fraternal affection for each other, not only because they had known each other for so long, but also because of the blood-tie, of which both of them were now aware.

Draining his glass, Beauchamp announced, 'And now Enid and I must be off. I've already got our luggage packed in the Rolls, along with all the other miscellaneous items I brought up with me, plus the bulk of your and Mr Hugo's luggage, so we shall get a good start, and find somewhere to stay for the night, as late as possible, so that we can make good speed to welcome you home.'

'Here's mud in your eye,' Lady Amanda toasted them both, and blew a kiss to Enid, who was so surprised that she actually ducked, as if a missile had been launched at her.

As the Rolls rolled through the imposing castle gateposts and on to the winding country lanes that would eventually lead to what Beauchamp thought of as 'a proper road', the inside of the car was alive with the sound of singing.

'Daisy, Daisy, give me your answer do. I'm half-crazy, oh, for the love of you,' rang out Beauchamp's pleasant baritone.

'It won't be a stylish marriage, for we can't afford a carriage,' Enid continued, an octave higher, and thoroughly enjoying this shared interest they had discovered.

'But you look sweet …'

At the end of the song, they both burst into peals of delighted laughter, and argued amongst themselves as to which number they should carol next.

By the time they were approaching an old inn to take their overnight break, their approach was accompanied by:

'O, o, Antonio, he's gone away,
Left me alonio, all on my ownio,
I'd like to see him now, with his new sweetheart,
And up would go Antonio, and his ice-cream cart,' a pleasant lullaby for them both after all the excitement of their little trip to Bonnie Scotland.

Back at the castle, Lady A and Hugo had managed to make it downstairs just in time for a refill of sherry before the first course, their appetite really whetted for the vintage wine that was on the dining table, the white, in an ice bucket, the red on a wine coaster, having a good old breathe.

From the quality of the food served, it was quite obvious that Cook had been let loose on the telephone to the local suppliers, and been allowed to order exactly what she liked, instead of having to keep inside Cardew's miserly budget. At last she could let her talents have free range, instead of having to work miracles with second-rate ingredients, and the results were superb.

Siobhan almost purred as she ate, sometimes breaking out into a contented humming. This is what life had been like before Cardew had cultivated his mean streak, which was probably when he had started squirrelling money away in the Cayman Islands for his escape.

The wines were not only wonderful, but did their job admirably, of loosening up all the diners, ready for some rather uninhibited dancing, after a suitable period for decent coffee, brandy and a little digestion.

As both coffee and cognac were sipped and conversation buzzed with the events of the last few days, the piper could be heard just inside the front door, inflating his pipes and warming up. While this was going on, some of the staff joined them, for Siobhan wanted an eight-some reel, and an eight-some reel she was going to have, come hell or high water.

Those from the staff perched on the spindly chairs that everyone else had avoided, and Siobhan, who was sitting with Lady Amanda, pointed out the variety of tartans they wore. Evelyn Awlle, Walter Waule, and Cook, Janet MacTavish were all dressed in the MacIntosh tartan, which was the house tartan, and had red as its predominant colour.

It must have taken a mort of tartan to kit her out, thought Lady A, but she looked good dressed in her national material, her face almost girlish, as she did a few cumbersome skips in preparation for the dancing. She'd make a man a damned good wife, she considered, especially if she could hook up with someone like Angus Hamilton. He might be a mite older than her, but they both had the same employer, and wouldn't have to make too many changes in their way of life, but could enhance each other's. Golly, she must be turning into a sentimental old matchmaker in her old age!

Mary Campbell was in her family tartan of dark blue, green, and yellow and with the application of a touch of make-up and a smile on her face, looked as if she'd just had her application to join the human race accepted. Sarah Fraser also wore her own tartan of red and black with white lines, as did Angus Hamilton, the chauffeur, about whom she had just been speculating, and whose tartan was very similar to the Fraser, but with a slightly less complicated plaid.

Sandy Gunn, the new piper, when he appeared, already playing, proved to be wearing the MacIan tartan, which was a dark one with a little red in its pattern. These last two were allowed to wear their own tartans, as they were not inside staff, as were the two visiting inside staff. Altogether they made a very colourful bunch.

Lady A and Hugo had not taken much notice of the other guests' tartans, as they had arrived just before dinner, in time to guzzle down a sherry and, as the first dance started to gather speed on the floor to the blood-stirring skirl of the pipes, Lady A and Hugo sat out with Siobhan, who wanted to share her knowledge of tartans with her Sassenach guests.

But just before she started on her explanation, she whispered to Lady Amanda, 'I don't know what I ever saw in that rat Menzies, and I've a good mind, now the entail's been broken, to put this whole bang-shoot on the market and make my home permanently on a good-quality cruise ship. Although I won't, of course, but it's a bit of a pipe dream, if I can't do something with the old family estate.

'By the way, the inspector found Cardew's fingerprints on your hip flask, as well as Macdonald's, so he must have stolen it from your room. Sorry. I'll return it to you before you leave,' then began to point out the different patterns of plaid.

St John Bagehot was in full Cameron fig, a complicated pattern with its red standing out against the darkness of the background. Drew and Moira Ruthven were cousins on their mothers' side, and wore the Buchanan, the yellow and oranges of which glowed like jewels against some of the blander tartans.

Ian Smellie's mother had been a Barclay, and they were both attired in the screaming yellow of the Barclay plaid. Siobhan, herself, wore the house colours of the MacIntoshes and, after all her identification of the clan colours, bade the two of them join them in a dance.

'But I can't dance,' protested Hugo.

'And I haven't done any Scottish dancing since I was at school, when we had this Scottish geography mistress who was mad about it,' pleaded Lady A, similarly dismayed at having to cut a Scottish rug. They had managed to do a little hoofing round the floor to look as if they were taking part, when there had been more people there for Burns' Night, but there were four less people now, their host being dead, and three of his guests arrested. Even Duncan

Macdonald was in police custody, and he had been an enthusiastic – not very accurate, but enthusiastic – dancer on that occasion.

'Come on!' Siobhan exhorted them. 'Angus and I will show you the steps at half-speed, away from the melee, then you can join in when you feel ready to.'

There was no way to refuse her, after all that she had been through, and come through more positive than she had been in years. Lady Amanda rose and held out a hand to Hugo, who was slowly creaking to his feet. 'Come along, old chap, you can't refuse the chance to say that you took part in Scottish dancing in a Scottish castle, on a Burns' Night visit, now can you? People will be so surprised when you tell them, back home,' she encouraged him.

Lady A soon picked up the steps she had not danced since childhood, but Hugo was the hit of the evening. Not really knowing what he was doing, even after some tuition, he allowed himself to be hurled and swung around the floor willy-nilly, whooping with a mixture of excitement and terror, as he swung at great speed from one partner to another.

In the middle of the Gay Gordons, which can be a very boring dance, he enlivened it considerably by getting himself in a tangle, when arm movements had to swivel the dancers to dance in the opposite direction, and it took two other participants, and a short break in the proceedings, to set him and his partner back on the right track, and facing in the right direction. He still managed, however, to make such a mess of the steps that, at one point, he seemed to be positively skipping.

After three energetic numbers, he retired to a sofa to become the elderly and retiring gentleman that he usually was, puffing hard to get back his breath. He was content just to watch the others 'cutting a rug', and noticed, as Lady Amanda had done earlier, that the usually surly Mary

Campbell, with the sheer joy of the dancing, looked less like a gargoyle and more like a woman, which he, personally, thought would have been impossible.

And that new piper was pretty much up to the minute. He'd noticed that, instead of a sgian dubh in his sock, he wore a mobile phone: rent-a-reel, 24/7. How modern was that?

They departed the following afternoon, leaving for the airport directly after lunch, with only hand baggage to take on the plane, as Beauchamp had taken all but their travelling clothes and their tartan with him and Enid, in the Rolls.

As they were on the point of leaving, Angus waiting for them by the car door, Siobhan thanked them for coming, and especially for their help in ridding her nest of so many undetected vipers. 'Don't leave it so long before you come back again. We've not had a Golightly at a Burns' Night since your mother died, and that must be twenty years ago.'

Lady Amanda forbore to correct her and, secretly never wishing to cross the castle's threshold again, bade her a fond farewell, adding an invitation to Belchester Towers whenever she felt like it. She then reassured Hugo, as they entered the back seat of the car, that she had no intention of ever coming north again. That was her finished with Burns' Nights north of the border.

When they arrived home, by taxi, from the airport, Lady A was delighted to see the Rolls parked ostentatiously outside the front doors, elegantly announcing that Beauchamp had, indeed, got home first.

Inside, there was a fire burning in the drawing room, the beds were freshly made up, and the smell of cooking wafted all the way from the kitchens, to tantalise their nostrils. Beauchamp had sorted the mail that had arrived in their absence, and put it on their respective desks, for

Hugo had been assigned his own 'work station' in the library, now that he was a permanent resident.

They were both, in different rooms, opening their mail happily, glad to see that Enid was there too, as she served them with a very welcome cup of tea. Say what you will about the facilities available on aeroplanes and in airports, but no tea tastes as good as that made in one's own kitchen in one's own home.

Epilogue

Lady A was just reading a missive from an acquaintance, about the approaching murder trial of her old friend Porky, when Hugo flung himself through the door, wailing like a banshee, and making little whooping noises.

'Whatever is the matter, Hugo? Have you won a chance to take part in a Readers' Digest prize draw?' she asked, with a little titter.

'No, Manda. It's Tabitha! My younger sister! She's coming on a visit. She's coming here! Do you remember her?'

Lady Amanda's face clouded over like a stormy summer's day, and her brows drew together in distaste. 'Do I remember her? Do I remember Tabitha Cholmondley-Crichton-Crump, Hugo? Well, I bally well ought to. She bullied me mercilessly all through school. That girl made my schooldays an absolute misery, and I was so relieved when she finally left, that I actually cried with joy. So, yes, I should say I jolly well do remember her, with no fondness whatsoever, and you've actually invited her here?

'Can't you put her off? Say I've got bubonic plague, or something similarly ghastly – smallpox, say?'

'Not really, Manda. She's arriving in the morning. It's just that we're a bit later back than we intended to be, what with all the palaver in Scotland, so she thought she was giving me adequate warning – I mean, notice. I'm sorry. But she is my sister. Do you think you could just grit your teeth and bear it for a little while? You can always come down with suspected plague if you can't stick it. I'm sure

Dr Andrew would play along, for the sake of a quiet life and a bit of a laugh.'

While she was digesting this bit of ghastly news, Hugo went back to his post and, it being later than it felt, what with the flight and everything, she was still on her own when Beauchamp came in carrying a tray with three glasses on it. 'Is it that time, already?' she asked, in surprise. 'I had no idea. Do you want to give Hugo a bit of a yell?'

'Not just at the moment, your ladyship. I have something of a private nature to discuss with you before Mr Hugo joins us, if that's acceptable to you,' he replied, mystifyingly.

'You're being very cagey tonight, Beauchamp,' she replied, feeling slightly queasy, having already had one unpleasant surprise, from Hugo, since their return.

Beauchamp put down his tray carefully on a small table, and Lady Amanda was horrified to notice that there was a slight tremor in his hand. Whatever was he going to say? He wasn't ill, was he; maybe with something incurable? He must be all right. He was her Beauchamp, and she simply wouldn't be able to manage without him, especially since she had learnt (and accepted) that they were kin.

'I wish to request your blessing, for I am planning to get married,' he stated bluntly, then just stood there with a poker face, staring at the wall above her head, and waiting for a reply.

Oh, my good Lord! He was going to leave her, after all this time! She'd lay money on it being one of the women from the castle. And she'd be left here, hundreds of miles away from him, with no possible replacement.

He'd be off back to Scotland, and she'd be left here all on her own – she had forgotten Hugo in her moment of great distress – with no one to do for her in the impeccable manner that Beauchamp had evolved over the great number of years that he had worked here. He wasn't ill at all. He wasn't dying. This was even worse, for he was leaving her, and he'd work for someone else, and not her, any more.

Her scream brought Hugo at what, for him, passed as a run. 'Whatever's the matter, Manda? You sound like the end of the world is nigh!'

With a face distorted with horror, she announced, 'Beauchamp's getting married!'

The words went straight over Hugo's head, or rather, their import did, and he casually asked, 'What have you made for us tonight, old chap? I'm dying for a change of cocktail.'

'May I offer you both a 'Goodness Gracious',' he replied, proffering the tray politely. 'I shall be having a 'Slippery Surprise.'

THE END … ALMOST …

COCKTAIL RECIPES

SNOWBALL
2 measures advocaat
¼ measure lime cordial
5 measures lemonade
Add all ingredients to an ice-filled glass and garnish with a cherry.
To turbo-charge, add a generous slug of vodka.

SCOTCH MIST
2 measures scotch whisky
Shake with a glassful of crushed ice, pour and add a twist of lemon peel.

GOODNESS GRACIOUS
1 measure cherry brandy
1 measure white crème de cacao
2 measures cognac
1 teaspoon egg white
Shake and strain into a glass ¾ filled with broken ice.

SLIPPERY SURPRISE
½ measure scotch
½ measure crème de banane
2 measures peach juice
2 measures grapefruit juice
½ measure passion-fruit juice
Shake with broken ice. Garnish with seasonal fruit and a straw.

HIGHLANDER
½ measure Drambuie
½ measure scotch
½ measure dry vermouth
1 teaspoon lemon juice

4½ measures dandelion and burdock or cola
Mix and add to ice-filled glasses and garnish with mint and a straw.

FROZEN MELON BALL
½ measure Midori
½ measure vodka
2 measures pineapple juice
1 teaspoon lime juice
Shake and strain over crushed ice and garnish with a melon ball and a slice of lime.

FROZEN SPIRITS
1 measure of vodka or other spirit, chilled until gelatinous
Serve in a frosted glass

APPLE OF MY EYE – Beware, non-alcoholic!
2 measures apple juice
½ measure blackcurrant syrup
1 measure pineapple juice
1 measure coconut cream
Blend with half a glass of crushed ice and garnish with a cherry and slice of banana.

ABSOLUTELY THE END! CHEERS!

The Belchester Chronicles
by
Andrea Frazer

   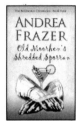

For more information about **Andrea Frazer**

and other **Accent Press** titles

please visit

www.accentpress.co.uk